"Why do you avoid me, mademoiselle?"

Margo looked directly into Paul's eyes. "If one doesn't wish to be clawed, one mustn't get too close to the tiger's cage," she retorted.

Paul laughed shortly. "Ah, the timid little spinster." His gaze was thoughtful. "Why are you not married? Are you frigid, or have you loved unwisely?"

Margo stared at him, shocked. "Why are *you* not married?" she shot back. "Have *you* loved unwisely?"

Raw little flames burned in Paul's eyes as he pulled her closely to him. He was primitive in his anger and in his intention. "You shouldn't provoke me," he said arrogantly. "Now I'll teach you never to do it again!"

VIOLET WINSPEAR

devil in a silver room

Harlequin Books

TORONTO • LONDON • LOS ANGELES • AMSTERDAM
SYDNEY • HAMBURG • PARIS • STOCKHOLM • ATHENS • TOKYO

Harlequin Presents edition published May 1973
ISBN 0-373-10005-1

Second printing May 1973
Third printing May 1973
Fourth printing August 1973
Fifth printing November 1973
Sixth printing July 1974
Seventh printing August 1974
Eighth printing February 1976
Ninth printing September 1976
Tenth printing February 1977
Eleventh printing January 1979
Twelfth printing May 1979
Thirteenth printing November 1979
Fourteenth printing March 1980
Fifteenth printing July 1980
Sixteenth printing December 1980
Seventeenth printing October 1981

Original hardcover edition published in 1973
by Mills & Boon Limited

CHAPTER ONE

THE hotel was in a Park Lane square, with a smartly uniformed man guarding the entrance, which was coolly shaded beneath an awning. If Margo had not already nerved herself to enter the place as if she had an assured income and a rich daddy she would have hurried away as soon as the porter brushed his eyes over her slim figure, clad in a moss green suit to compliment the copper gleam of her hair.

She tilted her chin and walked into the foyer, with that aroma peculiar to expensive hotels, a combination of deep carpets, scent and coffee, remembered from the days when she had worked in the flower shop of a hotel on the azure coast of France.

She approached the reception desk and spoke to the young man in charge of it. 'I have an appointment to see Madame Cassalis,' she said. 'My name is Margo Jones.'

The young man flicked his eyes over her person, and then consulted the appointment book in front of him on the marble-topped desk. 'Yes, we have your name here, Miss Jones. Your appointment with Madame Cassalis is for three-thirty, so if you will take a seat I will see that she is informed of your arrival.'

'Thank you.' Margo withdrew to the centre of the lounge, where arcades held small shops selling art objects, wines and flowers. It brought back to her memories edged with pain to see the tall baskets of mimosa and roses, flown all the way from the south of France for the delight of women admired or loved by a certain man.

Margo forced herself to relax in a soft leather chair, and she avoided the glances that came her way from guests who were staying at the hotel and lazing away the

5

idle hour before tea.

She opened her handbag and flicked through its contents without really seeing them; anything to keep her occupied until she was summoned to the suite of Madame Cassalis. She could feel the beat of her heart beneath the smooth material of her jacket. She wore her best suit for the interview, and a whisper of her favourite perfume. She was cool-skinned, and this helped to make her look composed. Her dark sheer stockings looked good on her long legs and fine-boned ankles. She took a look in her powder compact to make sure her nose wasn't shiny, for she wanted the job with a strange urgency which mustn't show when she came face to face with the mother of Michel.

She must be poised and cool, as if she were a total stranger applying for this post of governess to the little boy. She must be *soignée,* for the French people liked that, and any sign of nerves would betray her as emotional, and employees in French households were not expected to be the owners of emotions; they had to be efficient, polite but never forward; neat but not too pretty.

Margo's attraction lay in her slender figure, her copper hair and her monk-blue eyes. She wasn't a girl who laughed too frequently, or flirted with men. She possessed an innate reserve, and she was hopeful that Madame Cassalis would approve of this and employ her for this reason.

She gave a start as someone approached her and spoke her name. 'You are Miss Jones?'

Margo glanced up and found herself gazing into the spectacles of a dark-haired, rather prim-looking woman of about her own age. She saw a flicker of surprise in the eyes behind the spectacles. 'You are the young woman who wishes to see Madame about the post of governess to her grandson?' The accent was as French as the dark linen dress which the girl had on, with a chain bearing a small golden cross.

Margo rose to her feet and found herself a head taller than the French girl. 'Yes, I had a letter from Madame Cassalis requesting me to come to the hotel. I hope you don't find me too young? The letter didn't state a particular age, and I have lived in France before and have a fairly good knowledge of the language.'

'You are rather young, but then it will be for Madame to decide your suitability for the post. Please to come this way, Miss Jones.' The dark-clad figure led the way to the lift, and when they were inside and it was speeding upwards Margo felt the dark eyes looking her over, discreetly judging her exact age, her dress sense, and her disposition.

'Have you worked before as a child's governess?'

'Yes, in America. I have my references, Miss ...?' It was Margo's turn to gaze inquiringly at the other girl.

'My name is Dalbert – Mademoiselle Dalbert. I am the personal assistant to Madame.'

A term, thought Margo, which probably covered a variety of tasks, for she knew from her previous stay in France that women of the Latin *haut monde* could be extremely demanding. Mademoiselle Dalbert no doubt acted as personal maid, secretary and confidante, for there was no denying that she looked the discreet, even secretive sort.

Margo sensed that Mademoiselle Dalbert would be pleased if she didn't suit Madame.

The lift came to a smooth halt and the doors slid open. They stepped out into a quiet corridor and Margo followed her guide to the tall Regency doors of one of the best suites. They entered a small, flower-filled foyer, and almost at once Margo felt as if she were stifling, for the central heating was turned full on, giving a hothouse atmosphere to the lounge, with its carpeted floor, striped silk chairs, and pale marble fireplace.

'I will fetch Madame.' A thin, ringless hand indicated that Margo take a chair, and she was rather glad to do so. She felt shaky now that she was actually here and about to meet the woman who, without being aware of the fact, had been responsible for causing Margo a lot of heartache.

Margo stared at the flower pattern across the carpet and there swept over her the old feeling of pain and resentment. She felt again the painful dividing line, the rigidly imposed barrier between those of wealth and position, and those born into a modest household and destined to earn a living by working for others.

If she had been a girl of Michel's own class there would have been no need for their secret meetings. If her parents had been well-to-do, he would have taken her to see his mother and money would have bridged the gulf which lay between a member of the Cassalis family, owners of a chateau and makers of fine wine, and a girl named Jones who earned her keep as a working girl.

There was a bitter little twist to Margo's lips, for it still hurt to remember that Michel had left her to marry a girl chosen for him by his family. And when in a while she met his mother those lips of hers would have to be polite; not a hint of resentment must be allowed to show itself. She had been nineteen, he her first love, and now five years later, the Cassalis family required an English nanny for the small son of Michel, who had died when his speedboat had exploded while racing on a French lake. His wife, Maxine, had been with him. She had been badly hurt, and was now confined to a wheelchair.

A door opened, and at once Margo controlled her thoughts and composed her features as Madame Cassalis entered the room. Margo rose to her feet, and felt a little jolt of the nerves at the accuracy of her mental image of Madame. She was like a *marquise* of the time of the

French Revolution, her head of careful silver waves held high as she came forward to meet the British girl. Her eyes were the shrewd, clear grey of a person whose feelings had long since been packed into ice and preserved for matters of the mind rather than the heart.

'I agreed to see you, Miss Jones, because your references came from a household of impeccable status, and your name is so very English.'

'But I'm not—' Margo stopped herself. Somehow this was not the moment to correct Madame by telling her that if one's father came from a Welsh mining village, there was a certain magic, a gift for dreams, in one's soul.

'You were about to say something, Miss Jones?' Madame Cassalis spoke excellent English, with just a trace of an accent, but there was a slightly cutting edge to her voice that took away the charm of the accent.

'I hoped, *madame*, that you were impressed by my qualifications. I took special training in child care.'

'So I noticed. You were nineteen when you took up this type of career, and you are now twenty-four. Did you attend college?'

'No, *madame*. I left school when I was fifteen in order to help out at home.'

'I see. And what type of work did you do at that early age?'

'I worked in a flower shop, both in London and later abroad.'

'It is quite a change from selling flowers behind a counter, and taking care of young children. What made you suddenly change your mode of employment?'

'I wished to travel more widely, and I like children, *madame*.'

'You are young, Miss Jones. You could marry and take care of your own children.'

'Marriage does not appeal to me—'

9

'Really?' The pale grey eyes swept over Margo. 'I wonder why not when you are quite a personable young woman.'

'I prefer to earn my own living, Madame Cassalis.'

'Or could it be that you are ambitious to find a well-placed husband?' There was not a hint of humour in the grey eyes, only a look of worldly cynicism, as if this Frenchwoman had never believed that such a thing as love could exist between two people. 'Well, that is your business, so long as you do your work to my satisfaction, and keep your personal ambitions from intruding into the lives of the Cassalis family.'

'You mean, *madame*, that you find me suitable for the post?'

'Your references please me. I met Mrs. Van Arden when I visited Long Island some years ago. Her husband published a book on the champagne valleys, written by my son—'

Margo caught her breath and almost cried out that the Michel she had known had been gay and fun-loving, and had not seemed at all literary.

'You look startled, Miss Jones. Do you know my son?'

'N-no. I believed he was – surely I read in the news-papers that he had been – killed?' Margo was suddenly very pale, so that her copper hair took on a deeper hue, and her eyes looked almost dark violet.

Madame Cassalis stared hard at Margo, then she turned away from her and gazed from a window into the pale sunlight of the English afternoon. 'The father of Desi is assuredly dead, but I have another son. And at this stage of our interview, Miss Jones, I should like to add that you would be wasting your time if you tried to set your cap at my son Paul. He is confirmed in his bachelor-hood, and tied up with the family business. I should not wish an employee of mine to be ambitious above her station in life. Do you understand me?'

'Perfectly, *madame*.' The colour returned to Margo's cheeks. 'I have never yet given an employer cause for complaint on this kind of issue. I do the work I am paid to do, and I trust I do it well.'

'The child, Desmond, is four years of age. His mother lives at the chateau, but she will not interfere in any way with your handling of the boy. She is not – entirely well, and has her own secluded apartment. It is to keep her from worrying about Desi that I wish to employ you. You are acquainted with the Loire valley?'

'Not very well, but I have worked in Cannes and I can speak French quite adequately.'

'Yes, you stated this in your application and it is a mark in your favour, and the reason I passed over an older applicant who could speak no French. I would wish—' Madame Cassalis turned again to study Margo from her head to her heels. 'Would you mind at all, Miss Jones, if I asked you to tone down your appearance when you come to work for us? Your hair is an unusual colour.'

'My hair is quite natural and not dyed, *madame*.' Sudden anger leapt into Margo's eyes; the suppressed emotions battled their way to the surface and cracked her composure. This was the woman who had held the whip of finance and filial duty over Michel's head. This was the mother who had put her own desires before those of her son's. She had wanted the Cassalis name attached to that of another *ancien régime*, and in so doing she had ruined three young lives. Michel, so handsome and gay, was dead and buried in the family vault at Satancourt. His widow was tied to a wheelchair, and Margo could never imagine again that tremulous love and longing for any other man.

All Margo wanted now was to care for Michel's son, and because this meant so much more to her than the luxury of losing her temper with Madame Cassalis, she strove for control of her emotional Welsh feelings.

'The colour of your hair is unfortunate.' Madame shrugged her shoulders with the disdain of the moneyed woman who considered that employees should be so plain as to be unnoticeable. 'However, perhaps you will arrange it in a plainer style, and not colour your lips, or wear such fashionable shoes. A uniform will be provided for you, with a cap to match. Of course, if you object to these few rules which I make—?'

Margo swallowed her pride. 'Not at all, *madame*.'

Madame Cassalis stared at her, as if for an instant a flash of resentment showed in Margo's eyes. She was not a girl who looked subservient, and for a moment it seemed as if her suitability for the job was poised on a fine blade-edge. Then once again the Frenchwoman shrugged her elegant shoulders, as if Margo's temperament were of no matter and could always be dealt with, either by means of a reprimand or a dismissal.

'The chateau is in a particularly pleasant part of the Loire, but deep in the country, Miss Jones. Far from the activities which you might enjoy in your spare time, such as the cinema and the dance hall. If you have any doubts about being so far from these amenities then please say so before we proceed further.'

'I like the country, *madame*. I shan't mind at all if my social activities are limited.' Margo restrained herself from saying that she wasn't a dance hall girl, and much preferred the theatre to the cinema. Good music was her favourite means of passing the time, but she doubted if Madame Cassalis would permit the use of her small record-player, which her former employer had kindly allowed.

Margo could almost regret that she had given up her post with the Van Arden children in order to chance her arm with the members of the Cassalis family – but her love for Michel had been bright and hopeful, and she hated to think of his child at the mercy of this cold, aristocratic woman who would train him to put devotion to money and name before love of another human being. Margo longed to see the boy. She felt sure that he would resemble Michel, who had been darkly handsome, and with almost too much charm, so that his death seemed even more tragic.

'The boy's mother, Maxine, has her own nursing attendant, so you will not be required to be of assistance to her. She keeps to her rooms, poor child. Her back was injured, and she was also burned by the oil from the engine of the boat – Michel was going too fast, of course. Always he had to cram an hour's living into a minute, but my son Paul is of a totally different character.'

Madame examined the ruby and diamond rings on her tapering, well-kept hands. 'Paul has no interest in the gay life. He is devoted only to his work, and he regards Michel's son as the next heir to the estates and the business. It was at his suggestion that I applied for an English companion. When Desi is older he will be required to speak your language, but if his formative years are spent with a Frenchwoman he will find it more difficult to acquire facility in the use of good English. I must add, Miss Jones, that I am gratified that you speak so well – for a working class girl.'

'My father was a schoolmaster, *madame*.' Margo spoke with dignity, and she looked this cold, superior woman directly in the eye. 'He was Welsh, but he taught English in the village school for miners' children. He died when I was fifteen, otherwise I should have stayed at school and had a fuller education. However, I am not ignorant and I shall be able to teach your grandson his tables, and I known a little about poetry and music.'

'Excellent, Miss Jones.' But Madame Cassalis spoke without interest. She was patently bored with the interview and ready to bring it to a close. She went to the door and recalled Mademoiselle Dalbert into the room.

The French girl at once cast a look at Margo as if to see if she were being dismissed instead of hired. Her face, however, was in perfect control when Madame Cassalis informed her that Miss Jones would be coming to the chateau to take charge of the child.

'I will leave you, Yvonne, to give Miss Jones her instructions on how to reach the chateau and when she will be required to arrive. You may then go with her to the tea lounge for refreshment. I am going to finish my siesta. These interviews are so tedious and I am thankful they are at an end. Miss Jones, please give Yvonne your measurements so that your uniforms may be ordered.'

Without bidding good-bye to Margo, she went from the room, having unwittingly hired the girl whom her son Michel had met at Cannes, and whom he had courted as ardently as if he were free to marry her. He had left her while they danced on the terrace of a restaurant, to return to the Loire to marry the girl chosen for him by his family.

He had sent Margo an amethyst love-knot attached to a gold powder-case. 'My love is both as weak and as strong as this jewel,' he had written. 'Forgive me for snatching a little happiness with you. I shall always remember your sweet yet spirited simplicity, and I shall always respect your independence.'

And now, thought Margo, she was giving up her independence in order to be with the child who might have been hers, had Michel been willing to risk opposing the wishes of his mother. Margo had not known about his brother, and she felt antagonism stir in her for this man she had yet to meet. He seemed a very cold fish in comparison to Michel!

As the door closed behind the grey-clad figure of Michel's mother, Margo became aware that Yvonne Dalbert was studying her with open hostility. 'Has Madame fully explained the situation?' she asked, assuming the role of inquisitor now it was safe to do so, and because she had the advantage of being personal assistant to the *éminence grise* of the Loire chateau, set within its own wine terraces.

'I have been told the disadvantages of the position,' said Margo, 'in as far as they would seem to Madame to be so. Actually I never go to the cinema and prefer to walk or read when I am off duty.'

'What about male companionship?' Yvonne Dalbert looked Margo over as if it were obvious that she liked male company. 'At Satancourt we live a very exclusive life, but of course there are male workers in the vineyards – though M'sieur Paul would be bound to nip in the bud any flirtation which you might start with one of his employees.'

'I have not the slightest intention or wish to flirt with the men who work for Paul Cassalis,' Margo said icily. 'Now shall we get down to the business of when I shall be required to commence work at the chateau and the best way for me to get there?'

'Perhaps,' said Yvonne Dalbert, deliberately, 'you are hoping to catch the eye of M'sieur Paul himself?'

'Without a doubt.' Margo waxed sarcastic. 'I should not be satisfied with anyone less than the master himself. Tell me, is he handsome and charming?'

The French girl stared at Margo, plainly uncertain whether or not to take seriously these outrageous statements. 'You might as well know at once, Miss Jones, that Madame has no intention of allowing her son Paul to marry just anyone. He is the mainstay of the chateau and the winemaking, and I know of a girl who lived to regret that she ever saw M'sieur Paul, let alone loved him. Do you want to know what happened to her?'

Margo wanted to say at once that she wasn't in the least interested in the love life of Paul Cassalis, or in the fate of his *amours*, but there was a disturbing glitter to the French girl's eyes, an intensity about her thin figure which aroused in Margo a reluctant wish to hear the worst about this brother of Michel's. If she knew in advance what she was up against, then she wouldn't be taken by surprise when she met the man.

'Whatever the tales you wish to tell me, they will make no difference to my decision,' she said firmly. 'I intend to work at the chateau and I won't be frightened or put off by the character of Paul Cassalis. You appear to dislike him, *mademoiselle*, for some reason.'

A faint flush clouded the cheeks of Yvonne Dalbert and her spectacles seemed to intensify the glitter of her eyes. 'He is not an easy person to – like,' she retorted.

'But you said this other girl – loved him.' Margo was intrigued despite her reluctance to listen to gossip about the Cassalis family. 'Do you mean that she became involved with him?'

'It would seem so.' The thin shoulders lifted in a shrug. 'The girl worked for Madame before I was taken on, which was a year ago. They say she was pretty – and one morning she was found in the lake – quite nude, you understand. Did you know that the chateau is at the centre of a lake? We are quite isolated among the chateau wine terraces, with the water all around us, and tall willow trees that weep like widows at the water's edge. Satancourt is not like other places – very different, I am sure, from what you have known, Miss Jones. There are times when the chateau has a dark shadow over it. Look at what happened to Michel – and Maxine, with her scarred face. The scar could be removed; a surgeon has said it can be done, but she refuses the operation. Can you guess her reason?'

Yvonne Dalbert was breathing fast, as if these tragic happenings excited her. 'Maxine loved her husband to distraction. She will never love anyone again, and she keeps the scar as a sort of memorial. A penance, I think, for living while he died. A sad, strange thing to do, eh? For a beautiful woman.'

Margo thought of Michel as she had last seen him, clad in a crisp white dinner jacket, a dark red flower in his lapel. Smiling, holding her close to him as they danced to a nostalgic song above the rippling of the tide as it came in over the beach below the restaurant. Kissing her hair, he had made an excuse to leave her.

She had waited by the stone coping of the terrace, while the sea gleamed and whispered far below her slim and wondering figure. At last she had asked a waiter if he had seen M'sieur Cassalis. Yes, was the reply. He had been seen driving away from the restaurant in his car. Driving fast, almost furiously, like a man in a great hurry to keep an appointment for which he was already late.

She had wanted to hate Michel . . . she had tried to do so, but had soon been taught by her heart itself that once it quickened to love of a person there was no way to pluck out the roots of it. They were too insidious and had dug themselves into her heart from the moment Michel had approached the counter of the flower shop in the foyer of the hotel where she worked. Directly she had looked into his dark eyes she had felt a sense of excitement . . . a promise of ecstasy never fulfilled.

Now she looked into the narrow eyes of Yvonne Dalbert and she felt a sense of reluctance. She wanted to snatch up her bag and gloves and flee from this hothouse suite before she became too involved with the Cassalis family and their strange history. Escape lay just beyond that outer door; escape into the London she knew, far from the Loire, where the drama of Michel's marriage had taken place. Once she walked where he had walked, and saw the place where he had died, she would become a captive of the place and would not be able to leave.

She was young . . . she could marry and try to forget

Michel by putting in the place of his ghost the reality of a family of her own.

There was Ralph Owens, the kindly American businessman who kept writing to her ... and there was Don Foxley, whom she had known all her life and who was now a professor of history at a university in the Midlands.

She had a choice ... it wasn't as if she had to take this job at Satancourt.

'You look uncertain, Miss Jones.' There was a baiting note in the voice of Yvonne Dalbert. 'Are you having second thoughts about coming to the chateau as companion to this child of so tragic a marriage? Personally speaking I think an older, more steady type of woman would be preferable. One without too much imagination, and your air of independence. I think if Madame had not been feeling so jaded she would not have selected you for the position.'

It was the baiting that decided Margo. The awareness that Michel's son was surrounded by people who seemed unsympathetic. Even his young mother, Maxine, was wrapped up in her grief and her pain. And if she walked out on the job, an older, unimaginative and unloving woman would be found to take charge of Desi.

'I am quite definite about what I want to do, *mademoiselle*.' Margo was once again her composed and assured self. 'You have instructions to give me, and I have measurements to give you, so shall we proceed with these matters?'

Yvonne Dalbert shrugged her shoulders, but her mouth had a turned down look and she was plainly disappointed because she had failed in her self-appointed mission of discouragement. She flicked her eyes over Margo's sleek copper hair, and the green suit with its well-cut lines that complimented her slender figure. In her eyes there gleamed animosity ... and also the curiosity of someone who had noticed that each time Michel Cassalis' name was mentioned the British girl had almost flinched, as if from a whiplash to her feelings.

Needless to say Margo did not take tea with the French companion, and after she had received her instructions, she took a walk in the nearby park as the evening shadows were falling. She would not change her mind about going to France, but she could not help but wonder at the wisdom of her decision to go there.

CHAPTER TWO

COMFORTABLY seated by a window of the jet plane that carried her to France, Margo read up on the Loire and found herself fascinated in advance by this famous and lovely province on the south coast of Brittany. It was a place of old red-tiled farms, crusty white walls, and forests that sometimes concealed a castle. The valleys were clad with grapevines, and rivers patterned the landscape. There were tiny ports where the lobster boats put in, with houses from another century lining the cobbled quays. Grey granite windmills, the slated conical roofs carrying the four white sails.

This was the land of the Breton knights, where the families long ago had been as powerful as those of princes.

The old pride and self-will was bred in the bone, and Margo didn't doubt that she was taking on quite a task. She would not only be dealing with a small boy, but she would have his grandmother in supervision of all she did, not to mention the uncle of the child, for whom a girl had leapt in the lake that surrounded the chateau.

It was not a story she could easily forget, and some deep instinct, perhaps related to the ruthless ease with which Michel had walked out on her, told Margo that it was not a fabrication on the part of Mademoiselle Dalbert.

She gazed from the window beside her seat and saw that the plane was gliding down through the clouds and showing glints of the far-down sea as they flew in over the coast of France and headed for the airport at Nantes, where she would take the bus to Brit-Sur-Mer, and be met by the boatman in the employ of the Cassalis family.

Everything was arranged, and each stage of her journey had been paid for by her employers. They might, she thought, be sparing with their affections, but they were paying her quite a generous salary, and the uniforms which had been delivered to her a couple of days ago were smartly tailored if a rather subdued shade of fawn. The caps were starched bands in a matching colour.

Margo could not help but think it a strange twist of fate that she should be on her way to take care of Michel's son. She longed to see the boy, and yet she was apprehensive.

The jet landed with all the aplomb of a bird settling on the runway, and in less than an hour Margo was through the Customs and her passport was stamped. Her stay was provisionally for three months, but she was looking no farther ahead than today and her journey to Brit-sur-Mer.

When she emerged from the airport she felt at once the heat of a real summer's day on the coast of France. She smelled the foliage and heard the birds and saw the dust on the long bonnet of the bus that waited just across the road. She rested her suitcases a moment in order to remove the jacket of her suit. It would be extremely warm in the bus, and she was wearing a sleeveless apricot shift; she had hesitated about the sleek style and colour because of Madame Cassalis' injunction that she tone down her appearance, but for the ride to the lake she would at least be comfortable. There was time enough ahead of her in which to submit to the imperious demands of Madame Cassalis.

In the matter of her hairstyle she had looped the copper strands at the nape of her neck in a chignon that blazed darkly against the creamy skin of her Welsh inheritance. Madame would have to tolerate the colour, and a flash of defiance lit Margo's eyes as she swung her

21

jacket over her arm and bent to lift her suitcases.

'May I be of assistance to *mademoiselle*?' The voice was French and persuasive and masculine. Margo glanced up swiftly and met the gaze of the man. He smiled at her and his eyes flicked the fine pallor of her skin, which was such a contrast to her hair and her almost violet eyes.

'I've only to go as far as the bus,' she said crisply, in French. 'I am sure I can manage, thank you.'

'But the day is so warm and suitcases are a mere *bagatelle* to a man.' He was very persuasive, and every bit as charming as she remembered the Frenchmen who had strolled in and out of the hotel at Cannes. 'You look so cool, *mademoiselle*, that it would be little short of a crime to allow you to lose your poise by carrying heavy suitcases across the road. Do allow me to be of service to you? It would be most pleasurable.'

Margo, who had come to France with the firm resolve never to fall a victim to Gallic charm ever again, looked straight at the man, an obstinate tilt to her chin. 'Please don't pester me, *m'sieur*, or I shall be obliged to kick you in the shin.' She said it with perfect coolness, and she meant every word.

He looked taken aback for a moment, and then he inclined his head in amused admiration of her British independence. 'It will be terribly hot in the bus on such a day at this,' he murmured. 'I have my Citroën and I would be honoured to give *mademoiselle* a lift to her destination. I assume you are here on holiday?'

'You take the liberty of asking too many questions, *m'sieur*.' She hoisted her suitcase and stepped off the kerb in order to make her way to the bus. At once he fell into step beside her and she was preparing to tell him to buzz off when she saw the Citroën parked a short way from the bus, dark blue in colour, and well polished so it caught the sunlight on its bodywork. She knew in her heart that it would have been rather pleasant to travel through the French countryside in a car with the top thrown open, but she didn't know this man from Adam, and she wasn't risking another encounter that might lead to regret.

'My bus ticket is paid for,' she said. 'And so good day, *m'sieur*.'

'Won't you please tell me where you are going, so that I might call on you?' As she halted beside the framework of the bus, he stood looking down at her coaxingly. He was well-dressed and attractive, and probably in his middle thirties. He was obviously used to a warmer reception from the female of the species, and there was no doubt in Margo's mind that he took her for a tourist. Well, she was not going to enlighten him.

'Thank you for the offer of a lift, but I really can't accept it.' She made for the steps leading into the bus, in which several people were already installed, while the driver, his cap at a rakish angle, smoked a Gauloise and drew breath for the long drive ahead of him along the narrow, precarious coastal roads.

She climbed the steps to the bus and found a seat near the front, where the windows widely curved to let in the view. When she glanced from the side window the Frenchman was standing at the side of his car and gazing quizzically at her cool, slim figure through the glass. Again he inclined his head, and his eyes were laughing at her. Instantly she had the feeling that he knew all the time who she was. She frowned and looked away from him, and was glad when the driver took his seat and the bus gave a hydraulic wheeze as it moved out from the roadside and started on its run to Brit-sur-Mer.

From the moment she had looked at the driver Margo had expected a fast rate of travel, and she was not disappointed. She could feel the powerful thrust of the wheels on the uphill, winding roads, and she saw forests of pine trees flashing by, tall and densely green, and tantalizingly shady in contrast to the warmth of the bus. She found herself yawning and to offset the dusty dazzle of the road she took her sunglasses from her bag and put them on. Everything swung by in an eerie false twilight, but the illusion of shade was cooling and she settled back in her seat and tried to make her mind as blank as possible.

It was a sudden change in speed which roused her, and when she opened her eyes she saw that the bus was clinging like a green leech to a white thrust of mountain road, its engines humming as it crawled up the steep incline. Below the window where Margo sat the scenery was a dense mass of foliage, and she felt the tightening of the nerves in her midriff. The wheels of the bus were on the very rim of the road, and if the driver should make a single mistake, he and his passengers would roll over into that valley and fall all the way to the bottom.

But the notorious nerve of the French did not betray him, and soon they were over the hill and in the country of the vineyards. The hills were terraced with the vines from their highest thrust to their lowest pitch, blue-green, bloomy masses of leaf where the tiny, tiny grapes were coming into shape, searching for the sun, ready and waiting to burst with the rich promise of wine.

There seemed not a soul about. The vineyard workers were probably taking their siesta, as were the other passengers on the bus. Only Margo and the driver seemed awake and aware, and somehow she rather liked the feeling that she was seeing the Loire valleys in their natural state, without the hand of man in evidence.

Beautiful, she thought, catching her breath as she caught sight of the river itself, a glitter of emerald wending its way through this magical countryside. They passed through a village in the very heart of the sloping vineyards, a cluster of sleepy houses and a little church so lost in ivy that only its steeple showed.

So this was the vale of the Loire, where kings had their

retreats in days gone by; lovely keeps and castles where only the birds and the waterfalls disturbed the peace.

Margo could almost sense the history of the place, even as she felt the magic. And then as they travelled farther into the region she saw a wider expanse of water coming into view and she thought for a moment that they must be in sight of the sea. Then she recalled what Yvonne Dalbert had said about the vastness of the lake on which the chateau was situated, and she held her breath as she peered down at the sun-shot water and realized that down there lay Brit-sur-Mer, and soon she would be leaving the hot confines of the bus for the coolness of a boat trip across the broad, gleaming expanse of the lake.

Then the bus rounded a bend in the road and began to travel downhill, and far out, a mere shadow in the sun, Margo glimpsed the island on which stood Satancourt.

Fifteen minutes later the bus drove into the market square of this coastal town and came to a halt on the cobbles, in front of the houses which time had weathered but which fashion had not changed. As Margo stepped from the bus she felt as if she stepped into a past century. A heavy, hot stillness lay over the place, though she was conscious of the flick of a lace curtain at a window, the stirring of a cat in the deep doorway of a house, the blaze of scarlet geraniums on a balcony.

The other passengers drifted away, murmuring goodbye but not pausing to ask the stranger any questions. It was as if they took their time to accept outsiders, and Margo was too cool-skinned and slender and stylish to be one of them. They had an old-fashioned air. They seemed enclosed and secretive like the courtyards of their houses, hooded in dark shawls or brimmed hats against the eye of the sun.

Only the driver approached and asked her if she had rooms booked at the local hotel. She shook her head and told him that she was to be met by the boatman from the chateau of the Cassalis family. Perhaps he would be so good as to direct her to the boat jetty.

He took off his sun-glasses and stared at her. But it seemed that the people of this region did not pry into the business of others, no matter how odd it might seem to them, and with a shrug of his shoulders the driver escorted her to a narrow alleyway winding down between the closely built houses, cobbled and shady, with the smell of damp walls rising along it.

'At the far end you will find the jetty,' she was told. 'Their boatman is named Jean, so just call out for him.'

'Thank you.' After taking a look at the cobbles she was glad she was wearing sandals. 'I enjoyed the bus ride. We passed through some lovely countryside.'

Again he shrugged. 'The English are noted for their love of the country. It is just as well, for the chateau has not the reputation of being a gay abode. *Au'voir, mademoiselle. Bonne chance.*'

'*Merci.*' She gave him a slight smile, and somehow she appreciated his rough cynicism more than the suave charm of the man with the smart car who had tried to pick her up. She proceeded on her way down the sloping alley, grateful for the shade from the jutting roofs and balconies that almost met overhead, shutting out the sun, and holding in that smell of damp, aged stone walls.

When she reached the end of the alleyway, the sun leapt at her from the surface of the lake, where the glitter was like that of melted silver coins. There was a variety of boats beached on the sands that edged the lake, most of them with their sails furled. She looked for one that would be all ready to set sail, and saw a craft bobbing at the water's edge. She made for it, and now her suitcases were beginning to feel rather heavy, so that suddenly she stumbled over a jutting stone and almost fell. Even as a long shadow crossed her path in the sun that was dazzling her eyes, a pair of hands caught at her, handling her roughly but steadying her with their hard strength.

She flung up her head and her eyes were filled with the alarm of her near fall, and the rejection of being touched by a total stranger. She almost gasped aloud as she met the piercing grey eyes of the man, set beneath the thick crescents of totally black eyebrows. His thatch of black hair was rough and tousled, and there was a sort of menace to his dark features and the broken bridge of his bold nose. He wore a dark-blue shirt belted into grey trousers, and there was an almost frightening width to his shoulders.

He held Margo as if it would have been no effort for him to toss her over those shoulders, and though her immediate desire was to jerk free of his hands, instinct warned her not to do so. One look at the hard, brown face was enough to tell her that this man was not the sort to whom a woman said 'buzz off'.

C'est formidable! Even as the words leapt through her mind, she realized how alone she was on this strip of beach with him.

'*Merci, m'sieur.*' A resort to femine charm was all the weapon she had against him. 'I almost stumbled and you saved me. I am looking for the boat of Jean, from the island on the lake where I am to work. Do you happen to know him?'

Instead of answering her question he asked one. 'You are the person who has come from England to be the companion to the child? You are Miss Jones?'

'Yes.' Her eyes widened, and their unusual monk-blue colour was intensified by her surprise. She had worked and lived among people with money and she knew that the clothes this man was wearing were good ones, and also that the watch strapped to his wrist had a strap of crocodile skin. He exuded a tang of tobacco smoke that was far from cheap . . . it struck her that he must be a very well paid boatman to be able to afford tailored shirts

27

(they would have to be so to fit those shoulders) and the best cigars.

'You are Jean?' she said.

'So you are Miss Jones?' he rejoined. He let her go and his fingers seemed to leave their impression on the skin of her shoulders. He picked up her suitcases and without further words made his way to the boat with the spread sails and the deck that was unlittered with red nets and fishing tackle.

Margo followed and noticed that for all his height and the spread of his shoulders, he walked with a peculiar litheness, as if every single muscle in his body was alert and attuned to act without awkwardness or delay. When he reached the boat he tossed her cases to the deck, then he turned to give her a hand over the side. Once again she felt the grip of his fingers, and though the skin of his hand was hard and weathered, the length of his fingers was extraordinary. And now she noticed the ring on the fourth finger, with its seal set in the wide band of gold.

As she allowed him to assist her into the boat, she cast a look at his face, and had a sudden sharp doubt that he was the boatman. 'Who are you?' she demanded, and her eyes expressed her doubt, and showed also a tiny leap of fear. He looked ruthless enough for anything, and here was she stepping into his boat like a guileless ninny!

'Who do you imagine I am?' He returned her look with a flicker of scorn in his grey eyes. 'A hot-blooded Latin who can't resist your white skin and your deep blue eyes?'

'There's no need to be sarcastic.' A flush stung her skin. 'You just don't strike me as a boatman.'

'How do I strike you, Miss Jones?' He raised an interrogatory eyebrow and he looked very dark and hard as he stood there beneath the white sails of the boat.

'I should imagine you would have a far more useful occupation than boating visitors to the chateau back and forth,' she said stiffly.

'I can assure you, *mademoiselle*, that visitors to the chateau are few and far between.' He drawled the words, but he looked deep in her eyes as if to impress the words upon her. 'The boat is used for carrying goods from the shops here on the mainland, and I do assure you that it will take you straight to the steps of the chateau and will not deposit you in the centre of the lake – after I have slaked my notorious passions, that is.'

His words cut like little whips, and Margo drew away from him and felt sure that no employee of the Cassalis family would speak to her in such a cutting fashion. The man obviously didn't like her, but that was endurable as she didn't care for him. But his manner was far too high-handed for toleration.

'I didn't come here to be insulted,' she said witheringly. 'I know you aren't Jean, so you might as well tell me who you are before I lose my temper by calling you the rudest, most overbearing person I have ever met.'

'I am Paul Cassalis,' he rejoined. 'And now will you sit down before I cast off and tip you into the water and spoil that fashionably skimpy dress you are wearing.'

She sat down on the timbered seat from sheer surprise. So this man was the notorious Paul Cassalis, and though she tried not to stare at him as he cast off and stood at the tiller, she couldn't help herself. He was so unlike Michel that it was incredible they had been brothers. Michel had been fairly tall, but not nearly so tall as Paul. Michel had been dark-haired, but this man was sable-haired, with a skin so tanned by the sun and the wind that he looked swarthy. Michel had been handsome, but his brother was not even good-looking. At some time in his life that prow of a nose had suffered damage, and the deep cleft in his hard chin was set at an angle. His eyes were grey, and consequently they looked like ice set in all that angular darkness.

'I had some business to attend to on the mainland, so I decided to pick you up.' He spoke without warmth, as if she were a bale of goods to be hauled to the chateau. 'I trust your journey from England was a smooth one?'

'Up until now, *m'sieur*,' she replied meaningly. The boat was skimming the lake like a bird, and it was to his rough manner which she referred. She knew he would understand her. 'The scenery of the Loire is very spectacular, isn't it?'

'You like the country, Miss Jones? We are fairly cut off at Satancourt and it wouldn't do for you to feel – lonely. You are an attractive young woman, and it strikes me as odd that you should choose to come and work at the chateau as the companion to a child. I hope you are not running away from an unhappy affair of the heart? The boy has enough trouble in his young life without the addition of a jilted governess.'

'Of all the—' Margo was literally lost for words. She stared at the water of the lake as the racy bows of the boat cut through the blue coolness, and suddenly she thought of the way Michel had died. Her heart jolted. Why did Paul Cassalis speak of an unhappy affair of the heart? What did he know – or did he merely suspect that she might have known Michel?

'You were about to say, Miss Jones?' The question came drawlingly over his broad shoulder, and all the time the dark shape of the island drew nearer; larger than she had imagined, shaped almost like a crown, with the chateau surmounting it – like a jewel.

'I believe, *m'sieur*, that Madame Cassalis was sufficiently satisfied with my qualifications and my reasons for wanting to work in France without the necessity of a résumé. I take it she is the person for whom I shall be working?'

'My mother is in charge of the household, but it might be of interest to you, Miss Jones, to learn that I am the head of the establishment. I give the orders.'

'Meaning that you would be in a position to discharge me if I failed to – please you?' She injected into her own voice a note of sarcasm, as if it didn't really matter if he turned the boat around at this precise moment and took her back to the mainland. The last thing she wanted was for this arrogant brother of Michel's to guess how much it meant to have charge of Desi, the vulnerable, living link with the man she still remembered with bitter-sweetness.

'I shouldn't hesitate for a moment to discharge anyone who failed to do a good job of work not ungenerously paid for out of my pocket,' he said forcibly. 'You had better be as good as your references, Miss Jones. I have the reputation of wringing every ounce of wine out of the grapes that go to my presses.'

'I am not unacquainted with your reputation, *m'sieur*,' she replied, and though she spoke in a cool voice never before had she felt such a rush of antagonism. She felt like telling him outright that she knew he was the direct cause of a girl throwing herself in the lake. She wanted to ask him if he ever felt a stab of regret or conscience when he sailed his boat across the lake.

Then he glanced round at her, almost as if he felt the bombardment of her thoughts, and looking at his hard, brown face she felt sure he was as hard inside as he was on the outside.

'In another few minutes we shall arrive at the chateau,' he said. 'Be very sure that you wish to work among us, Miss Jones. My mother is an aristocratic woman who does not make friends with the staff, and my sister-in-law is a beautiful, broken shadow of herself. Myself you don't like, so all you will be left with is a child of four.' He raked his grey eyes all over her. 'Will it suffice for you? You are not the plain and dowdy woman I would prefer in your place, so what happens when you start wishing for

31

male company and masculine attentions? For someone to tell you that you have a delectable white skin smoothly arranged over a desirable body? And that you have hair almost the colour of the *noirblaize* – a rose which grows in the grounds of the chateau? What will you do, Miss Jones, when your loneliness overrides your sense of duty?'

She was thoroughly jolted by the things he said. It seemed almost an invasion of her person that he should speak outright of secret, buried desires – buried with Michel. It was like a ravishment to have this man's eyes upon her figure, and her hair.

How dared he speak to her in such an outrageous fashion!

'When I am capped and uniformed I daresay I shall look every inch the dutiful attendant,' she said, and she couldn't help but look at him with a residue of outraged virtue in her eyes. 'As for men – they don't worry me. There are such oddities as career women, you know.'

'I have known a few, but none of them had your looks,' he drawled. 'I am not saying you are pretty, Miss Jones, so there is no need to blush. I am saying that you have sex appeal, which is quite another matter. At Satancourt we don't cater for the heart. We are not a loving family, *mademoiselle.*'

'I had already gathered that much for myself,' she retorted. 'In which case it would seem that the child is in need of me. I shall, perhaps, bring a little warmth into his life.'

'I believe you might.' The grey eyes stared at her. 'You speak excellent French. May I ask where you acquired such facility?'

'As I told your mother, I worked in the south of France for some time, when I was younger. It was naturally convenient for me to learn the language.'

'You must have been very young, Miss Jones – a mere teenager.'

'Quite, *m'sieur*. My mother wished to remarry after my father died and it was a disadvantage to her to have a teenaged daughter at home, so I went abroad to work. I felt I was free to do so, and travel broadens the mind, so they say.'

'You are a young woman of initiative, eh?'

'I like to think so. In my line of work it wouldn't do to be a sort of Jane Eyre, would it? I might be taken advantage of.'

'And so far you have never had such a thing happen to you, eh?' He spoke sardonically, as if he expected her to agree with him even if the truth were the opposite to his statement.

'No.' She tilted her chin, and didn't realize that the gesture was defiant and that it gave the lie to her denial. 'And I don't plan to have it happen.'

'Wise young woman! Let us hope that your plans don't go astray.'

After that remark he gave all his attention to the steering of the boat, which was riding in smoothly to meet the wide stone steps that jutted down into the water, with an iron mooring ring attached to them.

Margo watched the supple ease with which Paul Cassalis handled his body and the boat, and she thought of Michel, who had strolled with a similar ease into her life and taken advantage of her lonely status as a British girl working abroad among strangers. He had flattered her, and courted her, and taken her dining and dancing at all the smartest places on the blue and gold coast of France. He had made life exciting for her, and then he had gone away and ever since a cloud had lain over her days and her nights.

Nothing could ever bring him back ... nothing could ever bridge those long months that had turned to years ... there had been no good-bye, and there could never be a reunion.

As Paul Cassalis moored the boat, Margo sat there tensely. They had arrived and soon she would set foot on the island and walk with him to the chateau. Soon she would see the child who would be a painful reminder of the man she had loved ... he would have Michel's dark eyes and he would smile with the same warm charm ... and he would never know that she might have been his mother if on one of those warm and languorous southern nights she had succumbed to Michel's kisses.

Supposing she had done so? He might have married her then, and he might not have died ...

'Was this the lake?' The words broke from her, before she could hold them back.

Paul Cassalis turned to look at her, big and dark, and. with features carved as if from teak. 'You speak of my brother, Miss Jones?'

'Yes – of course.' When she met the flash of his grey eyes she wondered if for an instant he had thought she was asking him a far more personal question, involving that pretty girl of a year ago.

'Yes, this is the lake. You would never believe that its serenity of today could have been the scene of a disaster, but this is where my brother was killed and where his wife was injured.'

The words caused her such pain that she had to look away from him in case the look in her eyes betrayed her. She saw the willow trees in their weeping attitudes at the lake edge, and she glimpsed the chateau on its rocky incline, its slim towers pointing at the sky, probing its blueness with high conical roofs.

It was a Gothic place ... lost in time, where *l'amour tragique* lurked within its ivied walls and behind its lancet windows, whose narrow panes of glass caught the sun on them so they gleamed through the ivy.

'Don't make me nervous of the chateau,' she said quietly to Paul Cassalis. 'I know you disapprove of me, but I have the spirit and the qualifications to work here.'

'Who said I disapproved of you, Miss Jones?' His eyes flicked her slim figure and her copper hair. 'I am merely concerned that you might find the chateau far from the amenities of your American place of employment. Not to mention your time at Cannes.'

Her pulses jarred at the significant note that seemed to enter his voice when he mentioned Cannes. Margo dared to meet his eyes, but they were unreadable, and it could have been her own sensitivity that made her so on the defensive in his company.

'I don't think I shall pine after the gay life, *m'sieur*. The chateau has an aura of romance which I am sure I shall like.'

'Romance?' he drawled.

'Historically speaking,' she hastened to add.

'Some say that it is aptly named Satancourt.' He held her gaze, and ever afterwards she would know how it felt to be dominated by a pair of eyes alone. 'Some suppose that I am an apt supervisor.'

CHAPTER THREE

SEEN at close quarters those slender, soaring turrets did not lose their aloof and fabulous beauty. If the many years and the variations in the weather had scarred the walls, then those marks of age and wear were cloaked in leaf, dark emerald patched with bright new clusters here and there, with lancet windows peering through like eyes that watched the arrival of the stranger.

Margo caught the plaintive chirp of hidden birds as Paul Cassalis escorted her along the cloistered path that led to the main courtyard, and when they entered she caught her breath at the unexpected loveliness concealed within the high stone walls. She saw the filigreed shadows of the sun through the boughs of the magnolia trees, with their tulip-like flowers a contrast to the clusters of rose-pink weigela. A huge vine was trained against a wall to form a *treille*, the green spread of it making an arbor in which cane chairs were set, companioned by a table littered with magazines, and among them an empty cordial glass with a straw left in it.

These very human objects were like a welcome Margo had not expected and she broke into a smile ... almost one of relief.

'I tried to imagine what the chateau would be like as I travelled here on the bus,' she said to her host. 'Somehow I pictured it as a cold, grey place, but instead I find it ivy-hung and very gracious. Aloof with its turrets, and that coat of arms over your doorway, but also a place that is lived in. I feared—'

'A museum?' he drawled. 'Or perhaps a prison?'

She paused beneath the tulip-like flowers of the magnolias, and the air was ripe with their scent as she gazed

36

up into the sardonic face of Michel's brother. If this man loved anything it was this old chateau, which must have been in the family for generations. The coat of arms was so deeply indented in the stone lintel of the door that it was almost obscured, and it seemed to her that Paul Cassalis belonged to those far-off days. There was about him an air of mastery, and a cloak of pride that was almost discernible.

Then in case he should guess her thoughts she ducked her head as a big bee flew close to her cheek with an angry buzzing sound. 'Come away,' said Paul Cassalis. 'The blossom attracts the brutes, and you don't want to be stung.'

She felt half tempted to ask him if he reserved that pleasure for himself, but she bit back the words and followed him into the hall of the chateau, with its high coffered ceiling, wrought iron chandeliers and fine old tapestries. Here was coolness, and great crusty-barked logs asleep in the fireplace, with its medieval chimneypiece rising almost to the ceiling and carved with figures and masks.

It was a place lost in time, haunted by its loves and its hates.

'Welcome to Satancourt.' The master of it all set down her suitcases on the fine old Persian carpet that covered half the timbered floor, worn jewel colours against the dark wood. 'I now have book work to do in my den over there, so I will leave you to be shown to your room by Berthe, the housekeeper.' He pressed a bell near the fireplace. 'She will not keep you a moment, Miss Jones. *Au'voir* for now. I will see you at dinner.'

'M'sieur—?'

He swung round to look at her. '*Mademoiselle—?*'

'Do I dine with the members of the family? I had the impression from Madame Cassalis that I should be no more than a uniformed servant—'

'As I told you on the lake, Miss Jones, I am supervisor here, and I don't choose to regard Desi's companion as a kitchenmaid. We dine at eight and I shall expect you to join us. We are also rather old-fashioned at Satancourt and we dress for the main meal of the day.'

'*M'sieur*, I think I would prefer to take my meals with the other members of the staff.' For some complex reason Margo felt compelled to argue with him on this point. 'I would feel more at ease—'

'Meaning you would feel uneasy in my company, eh?' The flicker of his eyes over her person held mockery, aided and abetted by the devil-black brows. 'I don't aim to make you feel relaxed, *mademoiselle*. People on their mettle please me better. I prefer lightning to serenity, so you will come to my table, and you will not absent yourself and make some trivial excuse. If you do so then I shall come and fetch you from your room. Do you comprehend?'

'Perfectly, *m'sieur*. And now do I curtsy in order to prove that I obey your order?'

His eyes locked with hers, holding the sheen of steel and the promise of a temper that would be like lightning, striking swiftly and not caring what sort of wound it left in its wake. 'Don't try me too close to the edge of what I will and will not tolerate from a woman, even one as attractive as yourself. Unlike other men you have no doubt known I can't be swayed by a smile, or tangled up in tricks. I hit back, *mademoiselle*, when provoked, so be warned and don't provoke my temper or my libido.'

She flushed, for there was no misunderstanding him. He would not spare her if she truly angered him, or aroused his other passions. He was ruthless, and he was master of this island, and he didn't care who knew it.

He turned on his heel and strode off across the hall, to an oval shaped door set deep in the wall. He ducked his tall head in order to enter the room beyond the door, which he closed firmly behind him. Yet so forceful was his personality that it was several seconds before Margo could relax from the tense position in which she stood. God, had she really thought of him as a cold fish! He was flame preserved in a wall of iron. He was steel from the forge still smouldering.

He was a dark, relentless man who made his mother seem in comparison like a pallid angel.

Then Margo heard footsteps and she turned to see a woman coming across to her from the direction of the stairs. She wore the long black dress of a housekeeper in a French household, with a white lace collar, a *châtelaine* of keys at her belt, and a knot of hair at the back of her head.

'You are Mademoiselle Jones?' Her voice was impersonal, but a flicker of the expected surprise showed for a moment in her eyes. 'I will show you to your apartment. You will wish to see Madame Cassalis in a while, but right now she is resting, and the boy is out in the grounds with Céleste. Please to come this way.'

She took one suitcase and Margo the other one, and they made their way up the dark wood stairs that branched off into three sets of corridors. Margo was taken to the very top of the chateau where, presumably, members of the staff were housed. Yet it seemed that she was being treated as fairly important, for she was shown into a bedroom with an adjoining sitting-room, leading into yet another room, where Berthe stood waiting while Margo took a look round her bedroom.

Sunlight came into the room from balconied windows, and the walls were white and relieved by small paintings and a shelf on which stood a Madonna with crossed hands and a blue coif and robes. The bed was big and canopied, as was only correct in such an old establishment. The clothes cupboard looked large enough to hold a shopful of clothes, let alone the modest wardrobe

Margo had brought with her. On the dressing-table stood candlesticks, and two big powder bowls also in blue china.

It was a room which smelled of linen which had been freshly applied to the bed after being taken from a closet hung with country herbs. It was not too grand a room, but all the same it was large, and over the timbered floor lay one of those colourful tufted rugs, handmade and tough enough to last a hundred years. Over the bed lay a thick crocheted spread which was equally durable.

In the sitting-room there was a rocking-chair, a small desk and a matching chair, a glass cabinet of books, and a fireplace with a tapestried screen set in front of it.

'Mademoiselle is pleased?' queried the housekeeper, looking as if she might frown if the child's governess was displeased. It was quite apparent that Berthe did not entirely approve of Madame's choice of governess. Perhaps she had hoped for someone of her own age, to whom she could quietly gossip, a little about the family, and about the ailments that Margo was obviously too young to have acquired just yet.

Margo smiled at her, hoping for friendship but not begging for it. 'I dislike modern rooms and feel they would be so out of place in this fine old chateau. It must be one of the best examples of chateau architecture in the whole of France.'

'It is certainly old,' said Berthe, 'and the many stairs can be trying to a woman of my age. However, you should not be troubled by them, and we have orders that your duties will be with the young master, and you are not expected to help with the housework.'

'I shouldn't mind that, Berthe, if you should ever need an extra pair of hands. I am not afraid of a duster, or even a broom, and I can make beds quite efficiently thanks to the nursing course that was part of my training in child welfare.'

Berthe stared at the slender, high-boned face, with a spirited directness in the almost violet-blue eyes. Then she swept open the door beside her. 'It was Monsieur who said you were to have this suite because of the bathroom attached. British people, he said, are inclined to like privacy in matters of the toilette, so here you are, and now I will leave you to unpack and make yourself at home. If you would like to come downstairs in a while, there will be tea or coffee to be had. Madame likes her tea when she awakes from her rest. Do you think, *mademoiselle*, that you will find your way all right to the lower premises?'

'I am sure I shall, Berthe. Thank you for the offer of tea. I shall love some, and I'm so pleased to hear that such an English beverage is available at the chateau.'

'Madame has a taste for it. M'sieur Paul is a coffee drinker, of course, and the stronger it is, and the blacker, the better he likes it. He is very much a man, that one. Very much the master here.'

'So I gathered for myself.' Margo smiled slightly, for it was hard to imagine Paul Cassalis as anything but the master. Strange that Michel had never mentioned him. Had they not been in accord? She could have asked Berthe, but thought it wise not to do so. She wanted not a breath of gossip or scandal to attach to this job she was commencing today. She wanted to make a success of it, and above all she longed for Desi to like her.

'Who is Céleste?' she asked, just as the housekeeper was about to leave. 'You said the child was with her. Is she one of the maids?'

'She is the young sister of the child's mother, *mademoiselle*. She is a playmate for him, but of course M'sieur Paul wishes that he should learn to speak English. I suppose it is necessary, as he will inherit, but he is still very young.'

The door closed behind the black-clad figure, and Margo was left alone to speculate on those final words.

Everyone spoke as if Paul Cassalis had no intention of marrying and having a direct heir. Yet he had struck her as far from being a cold-natured misogynist.

Was it possible that he had been enamoured of the girl who had jumped in the lake?

She had been Madame's personal maid, and it would hardly have suited that cool, proud woman to have her for a daughter-in-law. Perhaps the poor girl had thrown herself in the lake because Paul had been willing to be her lover but not her husband?

Margo couldn't help but feel intrigued. She hadn't dreamed that she would feel so strongly the forceful and yet enigmatic personality of this brother Michel had never mentioned. She hadn't planned to feel a sense of involvement in the lives of the adults who lived under the turreted roof of the chateau. She had meant to be impersonal towards them and to save her concern for the child. But already she knew that it would not be possible to remain detached. Her interest had quickened at the mention of Céleste, and the way Berthe had laid emphasis upon the fact that up until now the girl had been Desi's companion.

Now that Margo had arrived to take charge the girl might feel resentful, yet Margo could understand the wisdom behind the order of Paul Cassalis that his young nephew acquire a command of English. Especially if in later years the boy was to learn the wine business and become a director of it.

With a thoughtful air Margo unpacked her suitcases and placed her things in the capacious closet and the chest of drawers. As she moved about the room she felt the painted eyes of the Madonna upon her movements, as if even to an inanimate object here at the chateau she was a source of curiosity.

Before going downstairs she went out on her balcony to study the environs of Satancourt. She breathed its air which seemed to have a tang of wine in it, or was she letting her imagination hold sway over her reactions to this place? Remote, set apart from the noisy stream of modern living, with the passions of love and hate still strong within its walls.

Margo had sensed this from the first moment she had looked at Paul Cassalis. He and his family were not people to whom ordinary things happened; this awareness was as real as the terraced vines, a mist of blue green created by the distant effect of leaf and berry growing together. She could also see a plantation of young oak trees and guessed that Paul Cassalis went in for truffle-growing as well. She had heard – yes, she must have heard it from Michel – that landowners planted new oak trees each year because truffles grew at their base, among the acorns. And the climate for wine was said to be perfect for the truffle, one of the most expensive items on the menus of French restaurants. Margo recalled that she had once eaten truffles *à la crème* when dining with Michel. It must have been then that he had told her there was *truffière* at the chateau. Lightning fruit, he had laughed, which burned out of its path all flowers and herbs.

'Cruel and delicious,' he had added, taking hold of her hand. 'Like a woman.'

But it was he who had been cruel . . . and today she had met his brother and seen the Cassalis ruthlessness unconcealed by an aura of charm.

As she returned to her bedroom she realized the difference between the two brothers. Paul would never pretend an emotion he did not feel; he would never hide behind a mask . . . he was as he was, to be hated or loved or fought with on totally honest terms.

He was formidable, and though she strove to tell herself that he was a man like other men and could not do totally as he pleased with a woman, even here on his own island, she knew that she was fooling herself and bolstering her courage on a false hope.

Anywhere he would be a force to reckon with ... here at Satancourt he was in complete charge, and Margo was suddenly looking about her and feeling rather trapped. Perhaps she should pack her cases and leave before she saw Desi. There was still time, and they couldn't hold her a prisoner if she desired to leave.

She took a step towards the bureau, where only a short while ago she had laid her lingerie and the six pairs of honey-coloured tights she had bought in London. Immediately she was facing the mirror and when she caught sight of her own face she stopped short and gave a frown of disgust at her own cowardice.

She had never run away from a job or a person in her life, and she wasn't going to start now all because of a man's hard, brown, tyrannical face, and half-threatening note in his voice when he had said that she had smooth skin and a desirable body.

A flush seemed to go over all her body as she remembered those words, and she stormily told herself that if he ever laid a hand on her, she would scratch his mocking grey eyes out of his head.

She tilted her chin and walked from her suite with a gleam of resolve in her eyes. She would stay for Desi's sake, but that didn't mean that she had to like his uncle or bow down to his every autocratic wish.

She made her way down the long, gracious staircase and noticed the family portraits upon the walls. Paul Cassalis did not appear to resemble his ancestors; in all things, she told herself, he had to be individual. She followed the aroma of strong coffee to the kitchen, and found it tiled and vaulted, with an enormous stove, and a ceiling-high dresser hung with copper pans. Everything looked spotless, and in an alcove there stood a large electric freezer.

Berthe was busily laying a tray with tea things, and

chattering in rapid French to a bearded man in a striped apron.

'This is the governess,' she said, without ceremony. 'Miss Jones, I have the pleasure to introduce M'sieur Hercule, who cooks food as M'sieur Paul makes wine. We may at the chateau be a long way from the fashionable life, but we do not live on pea soup and pigs' knuckle.'

Margo had to smile as she held out a hand to the chef. 'I am pleased to meet you, *m'sieur*. How nice it is to see copper pans glowing in a kitchen. I like such things, though everyone seems to think that I shall feel out of place here, as if I were a dancer or a model.'

'You see, *mademoiselle*,' the chef's eyes twinkled beneath his bushy brows, 'you have not the kind of looks that one associates with a governess. You are *chic* and very charming. I, for one, applaud your addition to our ménage.'

'Thank you, *m'sieur*. Your coffee smells delicious, and though I came for a cup of tea I think I'll have coffee instead.'

He poured it for her and tipped in a swirl of cream. 'You take sugar, *mademoiselle*?'

'Two lumps, please.' She sat down at the table to drink it, and was delighted to learn that M'sieur Hercule had worked in London. Berthe departed with the tea tray for Madame, the silver pot and delicate china arranged with exactitude on the lace mat.

'Madame will be awakening from her siesta,' said the chef, who recommended his shredding with a sharp knife of long runner beans. 'I expect you are looking forward, *mademoiselle*, to meeting your young man? Have they told you he is a rather delicate child, with nerves on account of having a mother who shuts herself in her suite and who will not face up to life again? It was all very tragic, but life is life, and no matter how much we love the departed, we cannot share their existence. What do

45

you say?'

Margo stared into her coffee cup and she seemed to see Michel's good-looking face reflected there. She had felt his charm and his kisses, but Maxine had been his wife. It was terrible for her to have lost him, and a man would not understand that love for a woman was a spiritual thing as well as a passion of the senses.

'I hope I shall be good for the child,' she said. 'I know I am younger than everyone expected me to be, but I am well trained and I have worked with difficult children before coming here.'

'The little one is not so much difficult as bewildered and sad. He loves his mother, but she cannot walk with him, and she hardly ever bothers to talk to him.' Monsieur Hercule shrugged his shoulders. 'She was beautiful. Did you know?'

'I was told, *m'sieur*. They must have made a striking couple.'

He stared at her, his hands slackening in their busy work with the beans. 'Were you acquainted with him?'

Her heart gave a thump as she realized that she had almost given away her secret. 'I gathered that he must have been good-looking.'

'What,' the chef looked ironical, 'after seeing M'sieur Paul? The brother was attractive, yes, but a shadow of the big man. He has done many things that one, wrestled with the fishermen at Brittany, and trod the grapes from dawn to dusk. He learned about wine in all the small, tough vineyards across the land. He worked, always worked, but the other one – he played. Handsome is as handsome does, *mademoiselle*. Michel liked the soft boudoir, but the big man – he had his nose broken when he was sixteen in a fight over a wench, at a grape-treading, but he was saving the girl from a *vigneron* who had been eating his wine and not merely enjoying it. Paul? Women worship that one, or hate his soul for his eyes that see

46

more grace in the vine, more sweetness in the cask. Beware of him, *mademoiselle*.'

'I intend to,' said Margo. 'I have no wish to end up in the lake.'

M'sieur Hercule gave her an old-fashioned look. 'A second word of warning, don't ever mention that episode to him. That unhappy chapter is not for opening again. *Pas comme il faut.*'

Then with a frown the chef glanced at the clock on the wall. 'Berthe is with Madame a long time. They are probably discussing household matters, and the big man will be getting impatient for his coffee. You had better take it to him, *mademoiselle*. You won't mind, will you?'

She minded very much, but had to look unconcerned about it. After all, she was merely being asked to carry a cup of coffee to a man working at his accounts in his office.

'No, I'll take it to him,' she said casually. 'I shall slip in and out and he won't know me from Berthe.'

The chef gave his ironical chuckle and filled a large cup with coffee so strong and dark it looked as if the spoon would stand to attention. 'You know his den? It is just across the hall, where the armoured knight stands with his lance at the ready. A small conceit of the big man, but who can blame him? This family is a very old one – *ancien régime*.'

'Ancient pride and the arranged marriage,' said Margo, as anger caught at her. 'He lives in the past!'

'Is the present such a wonderland, *mademoiselle*? Only today I was reading in the newspaper – *mon Dieu*, we thought wars were over and done with, men of my time. We thought at last that the crying of the innocent could turn to laughter. Poor fools!'

Margo bit her lip. 'You were all magnificent. My father was in the navy; his ship was torpedoed and the oil got into his lungs. He was never strong after that, and he died before his time.'

'So live, *mademoiselle*! Don't let your youth lose its glow – don't be afraid to love.'

She smiled and left the kindly philosopher to his preparations for the evening meal. She made her way along the passage to the entrance into the hall and she welcomed the coolness after the aromatic warmth of the kitchen. Across the hall she could see the dim burnished gleam of the armoured knight, and a shaft of red sunlight came through a lancet window, and for a moment it was as if she had stepped back into the past and was a serving wench of the chateau carrying a flagon of wine to the *seigneur.*

She smiled at her own fanciful notion, but as she made her way to the oval door the shadows of the falling day were gathering in the deep alcoves of the hall and sliding dusky veils over the silk-worked faces in the tapestries that hung upon the stone walls.

How far away seemed London with its teeming traffic and its tall modern buildings, and the doubts which had assailed her there, the day she had been interviewed by Madame Cassalis.

Those doubts returned with a rush as she paused outside the door of Paul's den, and she had to brace herself before turning the ringed handle to enter. He glanced up briefly and the shaded light of the desk lamp cast his face in bronze; he seemed only to see the cup of coffee in her hand and he bade her bring it to him and place it within reach of his hand.

Hoping that he took her for one of the maids she did as he told her, and was turning away again, tensed to make a swift escape from this rather severe room, when he glanced up again and she felt the piercing rake of his eyes over her profile.

'How good of you to bring my coffee to me in person,' he drawled. 'I was just wondering where it had got to.'

'Berthe was busy, and the chef didn't wish you to be kept waiting, *m'sieur*. It looks awfully strong without cream – are you sure?'

'Utterly, Miss Jones.' He lifted the cup and took a deep mouthful of the hot, strong coffee. 'So you are finding your way about, eh? Is your apartment to your satisfaction?'

'Completely, *m'sieur*.' She echoed his own tone, in as far as she could, and saw his lip quirk. She glanced away from him as a funny little nerve quivered at the base of her throat, and ran her eyes along the rows of books, to the cabinet filled with miniature wine bottles, to the dark wood floor covered here and there by a skin rug.

A match struck, cigar smoke jetted, and again that nerve quivered and her hand rose involuntarily to hide that tiny betrayal of nervous reaction to him. He had called this room his den, and it was rather like being alone with a creature of unpredictable moods.

'You are looking about you as if curious,' he said. 'Is that why you brought the coffee? Did you wish to see this room, in which I spend most of my time when I am not attending to the vines?'

'You said you had accounts to attend to, *m'sieur*.' She turned to face the door. 'I'll leave you to get on with them—'

'I had just blotted the final entry when you came in. Stay a moment, Miss Jones. Sit down in that easy chair and let us discuss our mutual curiosity.'

'I'm not curious about you,' she protested, turning again to look at him, her whole being tense with denial. 'Why should I be?'

'All women have an innate curiosity about the single male – just as the male has to know why an attractive young woman is still unwed. There are two suppositions which leap immediately to mind, she is either frigid, or has loved unwisely. I am trying to decide into which category you fit, *mademoiselle*. Despite the dark fire of your hair you could be as cold as a statue. One cannot always judge by looking.'

'And why are you still a bachelor?' she shot at him. 'Have you loved unwisely?'

She had been warned only a short while ago to beware of this man, but he was so provoking; he seemed to enjoy setting a spark to her temper. She saw his eyes narrow until the pupils glittered in the lamplight. Dusk had invaded the room and the only illumination lay in a pool around his desk where he sat, so that each detail of him was etched in relief against the darkness. His thick black hair, wide shoulders, and jut of the cigar between his lips.

His immobility was unnerving, and then suddenly he was on his feet and Margo backed towards the door as he came round his desk and approached her with supple, silent intent.

'You will stay exactly where you are and not leave this room until I give you permission to do so. You won't run away like a little coward and not face the consequences of your remark.' His voice grated, and she froze where she stood and saw him remove the cigar from between his lips and place it in the raised groove of the ashtray on his desk. She saw also the glitter of his eyes as he followed her into the dusky region of the room.

Only once before had Margo felt this sense of doom, of consequences beyond her control, and that was when Michel had walked out of her life. Now his brother was walking into it, coming so darkly close to her that she felt as if she couldn't breathe properly. What was he going to do? Shake her, chastise her – but when his hands gripped her shoulders and slid down to enclose her waist, she jerked her head to one side and said the only word that her thumping heart would allow.

'Don't!'

'Don't – what?' he drawled. 'Show my anger because a chit of a governess presumes to judge me on a matter she knows absolutely nothing about? Retaliate in the only way a man can, short of a spanking – and that would be most undignified. The fact is, Miss Jones, I know enough about the female sex to guess that when a member of the species chooses to provoke a man she isn't asking to be spanked, she is curious to find out what his kisses are like. Deny this for all you are worth, but it's true.'

'It's far from true – in my case,' Margo said, made breathless by his closeness and by her fear of a situation beyond her control. There was a hardness to him that could break her, if he so wished. There was a ruthless, uncaring mockery in him. He didn't care if she hated him – it didn't matter a flick of the eyebrow to him if she left this house tonight.

He might even dismiss her, after he had carried out his threat to kiss her.

'Please—'

'I do enjoy it, *mademoiselle*, when a woman pleads with me so appealingly.' Suddenly his hand was at the nape of her neck and he was forcing her to look at him, pressing his fingers just hard enough into her neck to promise pain if she should resist him. She did attempt this out of sheer nervous rebellion, but his fingers gripped her nape under the heavy silk of her hair, and when she gave a little moan, he smiled ever so slightly, as if he really enjoyed tormenting her.

'Brute!' she gasped, and every nerve in her body seemed alive with a terrible awareness as he pulled her so close to his body that she could feel the beating of his heart. All that lay between her and the brown supple skin of him was the blue shirt he wore, which lay open to a dark cross of hair and a Latin medal that was warm against her from his warmth. He was primitive in his anger, and his intention, and never in her life had Margo

51

come up against a force such as his.

'You are such a sensitive creature, Miss Jones, that you should take more care when you attack a man like me. I am not only stronger than you are, but I'm tenacious. I never veer off a course, a subject, or a venture, once undertaken. As I said once before, you are very desirable, and you smell delicious – like a rose when its petals are slowly stripped from the heart of it.'

Margo could feel his head coming down to hers and a primitive fear of him rushed all through her body, chained to him by his muscular arm and his hand that gripped the nape of her neck. She had to fight back before that bold and mocking mouth touched hers – and she knew it was going to, at any moment.

She felt the warm rush of his breath and bared her even young teeth, and as she felt his lips she bit him, fiercely and deliberately, and his oath was her paean of pleasure. Now he would let her go – he must – but instead, almost cracking her spine, he bent her over his arm and she was held powerless as his mouth descended on hers and silenced her cry.

As the shock of his kiss vibrated through her, he taught her in a matter of seconds what she had not learned in twenty-four years. He taught her that her mind that hated and distrusted him bore no relation to her body. Its sensations were so acute, so physical, that she was alien to herself, not Margo Jones but some wild creature who hated and fought him even as she revelled in this sensual flame that rippled between them, around them, and filled the air with a hot, drugging scent of smoke—

'Bien sûr!' He dragged free of her and she was blinded by her loosened hair as he bent swiftly to the floor and lifted his smouldering cigar from where it had fallen to one of the skin rugs.

Margo stood a moment, thrust back against the door, while the smell of the smouldering rug filled the room.

Then as the realization struck her that she was free of his arms she turned and pulled open the door and fled across the hall to the stairs.

She was running up the stairs when a door opened and a dark-clad figure stepped out of a *salon* and a voice called her name. 'Mademoiselle Jones! Where are you going? Madame wishes to have a few words with you.'

Margo flung a look over her shoulder and through the copper swing of her hair she saw Yvonne Dalbert standing in the hall, staring up at her. Across the hall Paul emerged from that room of his, and Yvonne cast him a look that made her spectacles glint.

Margo clenched the balustrade of the stairs with her hand, and she knew what Yvonne saw with her sharp, curious eyes. She saw a man with his shirt half-open across his broad chest, and his black hair tousled above dangerously gleaming eyes. And above him on the stairs, like Jael caught running from the tent of the warrior Sisera, the girl who had come to Satancourt to be governess to his nephew.

It was a provocative moment, so filled with guilt and the flare of passion that it was almost as if lightning flashed in the hall.

'Return to my mother.' Paul spoke firmly to Yvonne. 'Tell her that Miss Jones has to tidy her hair and powder her nose before she is presentable.'

'Of course, *m'sieur*.' Yvonne's voice was smoothly polite, but there was insolence in the final look she gave Margo before returning to the room from which she had emerged. Her face as she went was tight-lipped and slightly flushed.

Paul glanced up at Margo, who instantly turned her back on him and hurried on her way up the stairs. As she went she told herself that she might as well pack her bag Yvonne Dalbert had guessed what had occurred between the new employee and the master of the chateau, and there was no doubt in Margo's mind that she meant to inform Madame that the governess had rather mistaken her duties and thought she was here to give instruction to Madame's son!

Margo pushed angrily at her hair, which Paul's hands had roughly disarranged. She told herself stormily that she would be only too glad to get away from a man whose instincts were as feudal as his surroundings. In his veins ran the old *droit du seigneur* attitude.

The right of the master to take whatever he desired!

CHAPTER FOUR

THE order came for Miss Jones to present herself to Madame Cassalis just half an hour before dinner was due to be served. Margo had bathed and made herself presentable, well aware that she would be summoned for this interview before the evening was over.

She wore her simplest dress and her hair was coolly looped at the nape of her neck. She wanted to look as poised as possible when Madame Cassalis told her that she was not required after all to have charge of the child of the house.

Margo told herself that she would accept her dismissal with all the dignity which Paul Cassalis had tried to crush, as he had crushed her in his arms. As she followed one of the maids downstairs it seemed to her that his behaviour had been calculated not only to destroy her desire to stay, but had been meant to make her look irresponsible. She set her chin and braced her spine as the maid tapped upon an imposing door, and then stepped aside for her to enter the *salon*, whose crystal chandeliers played their light over the silk-striped chairs and sofas in carved frames, and the paintings of gracious figures in wigs and silk.

Madame Cassalis was waiting for her, wearing a pearl-grey dress with a cameo at the throat, her thin patrician figure so upright against the sweeping folds of the white brocade curtains tied with silver tassels.

She did not speak directly but stared at Margo with a flicker of contempt in her pale, cold eyes. There rushed through Margo a wild desire to be free of this family ... she wished with all her heart that she had never come here, and never imagined that she could give affection and warmth of heart to Michel's little boy. She wanted to escape and was nervously strung to say to Madame that she didn't require a lecture and was prepared to leave Satancourt tonight, if Jean the boatman would be good enough to take her across the lake.

'So, Miss Jones, you appear to think that you came here in order to be the companion of my son rather than my grandson. It this true?'

The words came so suddenly, so coldly, that Margo gave a nervous jump and felt snatched from her the advantage of proffering her notice. She swallowed the dryness from her throat, and hated it that she felt so guilty when all the time she was innocent. She had to defend herself. It was unfair that she be regarded as a sort of Jezebel while *he* was treated as if he were St. Paul led astray by *her* advances.

'I am sure Mademoiselle Dalbert has exaggerated the scene which she witnesed in the hall, *madame*.' Margo tried to keep her voice as coolly controlled as possible. 'The truth is that your son doesn't wish me to stay and have charge of your grandson. I am certain he would like me to leave so he can hire a governess much older than I and with a meeker disposition. If this type of person was required in the first place, then I should have been told in London before making this long journey to the chateau.'

'I think we are talking at cross purposes, Miss Jones.' A thin smile came and went on Madame's lips, while the grey eyes dwelt meaningly on Margo's mouth. 'Yvonne tells me that you had obviously been in my son's arms, and men hardly demonstrate their disapproval of a woman by embracing her. I can but assume that you encouraged him to behave in this way.'

'I most certainly did not!' Margo drew herself up very straight, and felt a burning sensation over her cheekbones. 'Quite frankly, *madame*, I find your son an arrogant, demanding man who likes everything his own way. Yes, he kissed me, but only because he knew I would find it intolerable to remain here after such an – indignity.'

'An indignity, Miss Jones?' The woman in grey looked even icier, as if never in her life before had she been told to her face that a member of her ancient family was not a paragon of all the virtues.

'Yes, *madame*. I have my reputation as a governess to consider, and I don't throw myself at the head of the family the moment I arrive to begin my work. I should soon find myself looking for another mode of employment if I was that type of person. You know the truth as well as I do, *madame*. Your son was aware that I had signed a contract to work here for three months, so he knew he couldn't dismiss me out of hand. He chose instead to discredit me in your eyes and so make it impossible for me to remain here. After all, how could you place a small boy in the care of a governess with doubtful principles? And what is the word of a mere governess against that of the *seigneur* of the establishment?'

Margo tilted her chin with offended pride, and the silvery glow of the overhead chandelier played over her hair and seemed to make it blaze darkly against her skin. 'I am prepared to give in my notice if that is what you wish, *madame*. But I hope you will make it plain to the association which places me in employment that I was not dismissed for misconduct.'

'You would not wish to return to selling flowers, is that it?' Madame Cassalis had been pricked and now it was her turn to thrust in the pin.

'I wouldn't wish to be labelled a Jezebel,' Margo rejoined.

'No?' Madame Cassalis raised an eyebrow. 'I believe she had your coloured hair, did she not?'

'I think my colouring is irrelevant to the situation, *madame*.' Margo was inwardly trembling, for never in

57

her life had she met people who were so overriding in their pride that a mere whisper of criticism could make them so cruel. 'If I am to leave, then I had better go tonight—'

'No, Miss Jones, you will stay. I have decided that you will do very well here, and be most suitable to take care of my grandson.'

'But I no longer wish to stay, *madame*.' Margo thought of facing Paul Cassalis again and could hardly endure the image of it even in her mind. 'I don't think the post would be a satisfactory one for me.'

'Nonsense, girl.' Madame Cassalis waved away the idea with the chiffon handkerchief which she held, and a breath of Guerlain perfume wafted from the pearly material. 'You are trained and capable, even if you are a young woman, and it would be a bother, a nuisance for me to have to go through the tedium of interviewing applicants all over again. They are not easy to find these days. They insist on television sets in their rooms, if they are older women, and the young ones are not keen on the countryside. I will confess that Yvonne – well, you understand, Miss Jones. She is very much the spinster and was shocked by what she saw. I am willing to take you at your word—'

'That is generous of you, *madame*, but all the same—'

'We will have no buts, Miss Jones. I have made up my mind, and I insist upon holding you to the contract between us. And now,' Madame Cassalis glanced at the gilt and mosaic clock on the marble mantelpiece, 'it is almost time to dine. You had something else to say, Miss Jones?'

'Your son will not be pleased if I stay.'

'No, perhaps not.' Madame actually smiled. 'But you and he will not meet so very often. He has his work among the vines, and you have yours, and in a few days he will be treating you as if you are a piece of furniture and all will be – serene. Just remember in future not to find yourself placed in a situation where you are alone with him and defenceless against his arrogance, as you call it. I warned you in London that my son Paul is not a man who goes in for the charming of women. He regards the procedure as a waste of time.'

Strangely enough these words caused Margo to smile. There was little doubt that Paul Cassalis wasted time employing the subtle interplay which had been part of Michel's technique in winning a girl's confidence. Paul attacked, and if his victim ran away, then he shrugged his broad shoulders and got on with his work.

Well, it looked as if she wasn't going to be allowed to run away, but for the life of her she couldn't face seeing him again tonight.

'Very well, *madame*, I am willing to forget what happened, but I should like to have dinner in my room, if I may? I am feeling rather exhausted. It has been a long day—'

'You will eat in the servants' hall, of course.' Madame Cassalis gave her a severe look, not untinged with curiosity. 'Berthe grumbles enough about the stairs without the staff taking it into their heads they can enjoy the luxury of being served meals in their rooms. You mustn't imagine, Miss Jones, that your position as governess to Desi places you on a different footing from the other – servants.'

'I don't imagine for one moment that I am any different.' The last traces of a smile vanished from Margo's eyes, and she actively flinched, as if this woman with the cold grey eyes had applied a whip to her skin. 'M'sieur Paul implied that I should sit at the family dining table, but I would naturally prefer to be with the other members of the staff.'

'M'sieur was teasing you yet again, Miss Jones. Only

59

Yvonne is in a position to eat meals with the family – and only because she happens to be distantly related to us. You know your way to the staff quarters, I take it?'

'Yes, *madame.*'

'Then you will join them, and in future you will wear the uniform which was provided for you.'

'As you request, *madame.*'

'As I direct, Miss Jones.' Madame Cassalis gestured at the door, and as Margo turned away and left the *salon* she had the cold feeling that Madame Cassalis was staring after her and disliking everything about her. It was only because she didn't want the bother of hiring another governess for her grandson that she insisted on Margo remaining at the chateau. As Margo crossed the hall she saw the darkness beyond the windows and she caught the sound of the waves rustling across the surface of the lake. The tide at sea would be on the turn and it would affect the currents of the lake. Margo thought of the willows and the clustering green reeds, and a girl's hair floating there, holding her to the reeds in the shallows of the water.

She had almost reached the baize door that led to the kitchen quarters when a tall figure turned from gazing out of a window in one of the shadowy alcoves. He was dressed in dark evening wear that made him seem taller than ever, his linen was crisp and white against the suiting, and his hair was thick and groomed above the quick stab of his eyes, holding her motionless as she was about to open the baize door.

He looked every inch the French aristocrat about to go and dine, and even as Margo stared at him it seemed barely possible that this civilized human being could have behaved as he had done, dragging her into his arms and forcing her to respond to his kisses.

A tremor ran all through her – he had not only forced her to endure his hands and his lips, but he had been the direct cause of that inquisition she had just endured from his mother. Hatred stormed through her body and found its way to her eyes, and she could hardly bear him to look at her, for he knew, as she knew, that an unholy sort of passion had flared between them and it could never be forgotten, it must always leap again at the edges of the senses whenever they met, whenever they spoke together.

'I hope it pleases you, *m'sieur*, that your mother has just chastised me as if I were some scullerymaid. But if you hoped I'd be on my way from Satancourt, dismissed by your mother, then you must brace yourself for a disappointment. Madame wishes me to stay.'

'Does she?' His eyes seemed mocking through the black smokiness of his lashes. 'Did you convince her that you and I have a mutual aversion to each other? How clever of you, Miss Jones! I should not have taken you for the subtle inventress of the convenient lie.'

'I'm not a liar,' Margo flashed. 'Every word I spoke to your mother happens to be the truth. You – you are the one who dislikes hearing the truth. Because I said something that hit close to a nerve you chose to discredit me by – making love to me.'

'I kissed you, *mademoiselle*.' His voice sank deep in his throat, and the lids of his eyes seemed to meet lazily, menacingly. 'If I ever made love to you—'

'Stop it!' Margo was gripping the handle of the baize door so forcibly that she broke a fingernail. 'You are all alike in this family, you care nothing about the feelings of other people. *You* use your position to ride roughshod over everyone – while your—' There she broke off just in time, before she spoke the fatal words clamouring at her lips. She had almost spoken Michel's name. She had almost revealed her knowledge of him, her love of him, and the pain she had suffered after he had charmed his way into her heart and then left her, without a word of explanation, in order to marry Maxine.

'I am already too well acquainted with the Cassalis virtues and vices to need your résumé, *mademoiselle*. So you believe I kissed you in order to make you appear – wanton? But may I remind you that you dashed from my den as if you were about to be ravished. I did not arrange for my mother's *confidante* to be in the hall, to witness the disarray of your attractive person.'

'If you hadn't touched me there would have been no such scene for Mademoiselle Dalbert to witness.'

'You provoked me, *mademoiselle*. I warned you it could be – inflammatory.' And as he used that word something seemed to smoulder in his eyes, raw little flames, reminding her of those burning moments in his arms. 'If you don't wish to be clawed, then you shouldn't go so close to the bars of the tiger's cage.'

The derisive look he was giving her was fuel to her fury, and anything might have been said, anything could have been said, had someone not come running down the stairs at that moment. Seeing Paul, the girl ran to him with such a trusting innocence and affection that Margo wanted to cry out to her: 'Don't trust him so! He is like a tiger. He purrs before he pounces.'

The girl hugged his arm and stared at Margo. She was about seventeen and her hair was smooth and dark, a silky cape about her shoulders, and there was an impertinent tilt to her young nose. She wore a dress to her ankles, and her slim throat was exposed by the rounded neckline, with the thin chain of a gold heart against her soft, almost olive skin. She was pretty in the unformed way of a girl not long out of the schoolroom. But her instincts were awakening, for she pressed close to the tall, hard frame of Paul Cassalis as she studied Margo.

'You must be the English governess for Desi,' she said. 'I thought you would be middle-aged and comfortably stout. You are neither of those things, are you?'

'No,' said Margo, and because the girl was young and innocent and not to be blamed for liking a man who no doubt treated her as an uncle would, a smile touched Margo's lips. 'I think you must be Céleste. Am I right?'

The girl gave a slight shrug and was not going to be coaxed into friendship too readily. 'I could have gone on looking after Desi. I told Paul so, but he wouldn't listen.' She glanced up at him and her dark eyes seemed to fill themselves with his hard, brown face. 'He is a tyrant when he chooses. He has to have his way or the turrets tremble.'

A smile touched his lips, then he glanced again at Margo. 'Where are you going, by the way? The dining-room is not in that direction. and I can see you are dressed for dinner.'

'I am to eat in the staff hall, m'sieur.' Margo spoke in her coolest voice. 'I will go now—'

'You will stay, Miss Jones.' His voice seemed to cut away the distance between them and a whiplash seemed to stir against her skin. 'I told you earlier on that you would sit at the family table and I will not have my orders countermanded by you—'

'It was your mother who instructed me to eat with the staff, m'sieur.'

'Was it really? But did I not also tell you that I am in charge here and my orders take precedence over those issued by other members of the family?'

'Yes, you did say that, but—'

'It suits you better to obey my mother on this matter. What is it, Miss Jones, do you think yourself superior to us? Do you imagine our table talk would bore you?'

'Of course that isn't the reason.' A flush stung her cheeks, and she was aware of Céleste absorbing every word, every intonation of this exchange, glancing from his face to Margo's with a gleam of excitement in her eyes.

'Then I will have the reason, if you don't mind?' he said. 'Come, out with it.'

'Madame is right, I am only a servant, a member of the staff, and I shall feel more at ease if I take my meals in the staff hall.'

'Very well,' he said, 'tonight I will let you off, but in future you will eat with us and you will disregard this nonsense about your status. As the governess of my nephew I shall expect you to dine with us, to sit in the *salon* afterwards, and to absorb all that is discussed in this matter of wine culture. I wish the child to grow up with the idea that he is to be a *vigneron*, not a playboy, do you understand? It will be part of your duty to drum this notion into his young head. Do I make myself perfectly clear, Miss Jones?'

'As a bell, *m'sieur*.' She couldn't resist saying this, and saw his black left eyebrow take its arch. 'Then for tonight will it be all right if I take a tray to my room? I don't wish to be waited on, but I am feeling rather tired, and if I eat in my room tonight it won't look so strange if I come to your table tomorrow night.'

'So with others you can be diplomatic,' he drawled. 'Only with me do you have to be rebellious. Very well, do as you wish – tonight. Go and see Desi after you have eaten. He will be in his nursery suite and the sooner the two of you meet the better. He has the Cassalis charm – which I haven't – so once he has you hooked you will be less ready to leap and run every time I look at you. *Au'voir* for now, Miss Jones.'

'Good night, *m'sieur*.' As Margo hurried through the baize door she heard Céleste give a muffled laugh and say something. Margo gave a rueful smile. They were all high-handed and full of themelves here at Satancourt. It was being so isolated, perhaps, the occupants of the chateau enclosed by water, by twisted pine trees, and the high terraces of wine grapes. The modern world did not intrude, and Margo, being a member of that modern world, had to adjust to the feudal atmosphere on the island or find herself continuously in hot water.

She collected her tray from the kitchen and carried it to her room via the back stairs, and how good it felt when she was alone at last, free to close the curtains and shut out the dark gleam of the lake through the trees, to set her dinner out on the small table in the sitting-room and relax at last from the strain of coping with the members of this household.

There was *crème d'asperges* in an earthenware bowl, with French bread, and so delicious that she didn't leave a drop. A *filet mignon* with crisp cooked onions and fried potatoes. Then stoned black cherries with a custard *mousse*, followed by a glass of wine.

Enjoyed in the privacy of her room the meal was both tasty and satisfying. How very much she would have preferred this privacy each evening to come, but she had been told very firmly that she was not her own mistress in the matter and must do as Paul Cassalis demanded. Well, Madame Cassalis would not be pleased, nor would Yvonne Dalbert, and Margo felt her nerves tighten again as she pictured the evenings that lay ahead of her.

What had she taken on? She must have been crazy to leave the up-to-date comfort and attitude of the Van Arden household in order to come here. The children had been a pleasure to take care of. She had made friends there at Long Island, and been allowed to have music in her room, and even the use of one of the family cars. There had been a pool in the large garden, and the amenity of a local theatre.

Yes, she must have been quite crazy, and with a sigh she rose to her feet and went out on to the dark balcony. She could smell the scents of the lake, the aroma of the pine trees, and high overhead she could see the stars in great clusters against the dense velvet of the sky. She felt the mystery and the beauty of the island, but she felt the sadness, too. She had hoped to feel closer to Michel by coming here, but now she could not imagine him here. He had seemed more a part of the gaiety of Cannes, clad in a crisp white dinner jacket, or beach trunks, teaching her that all duty and no play made life very dull.

Well, it looked as if the philosophy of Paul Cassalis was very much the opposite to this. He obviously believed that duty took precedence over everything else, and even the child was to be taught as early as possible that his duty lay in the family business and he must be modelled after his uncle rather than his father.

A stab of rebellion made Margo clench her hands over the ironwork of the balcony. Desi was only four and she'd be darned if she would drum into him the *habitude* of duty before he was out of short breeches.

Her eyes dwelt broodingly on the stars ... somewhere up there the gay spirit of Michel still shone on. She who had loved him, with her very youthful heart, could not condemn him for wringing every ounce of delight from life. He had known, even as they had danced together, that the hand of family duty lay upon his shoulder in the guise of the arranged marriage.

It was all too Latin, too proud and primitive a practice for Margo to fully understand how a man could leave someone he really wanted to become the husband of a woman selected for him, forced upon him by the dictates of a proud mother and an older brother too bound up in his precious vines to spare the time for a wife.

Strange, really, that Paul should wish to pass all this on to a nephew rather than a son of his own. It was really a wonderful old place, aromatic with its plants and creepers established over the long years, alive in all its stones with the drama and history of its long life. Here had the love and violence of its ancestors been played out, against a background of romantic turrets and dim cloisters where the passion-vine climbed and clung and gave out its sensuous scent. A man could not live within these walls and be master of them without feeling love of the place in his very bones. Therefore how strange, how complex, that he should denounce marriage for himself and plan to pass on his heritage to his brother's child.

Margo thought of the way Céleste had clung to his arm and stared at his face with eager eyes. She thought of the girl in the lake and when suddenly a low animal shriek ran through the foliaged darkness below her balcony, she retreated with a little gasp, as if claws were at her throat.

Margo drew the curtains quickly on that painful sound, that reminder from out of the night that ruthlessness was part of nature and the chateau was surrounded by the forces of nature.

She stacked her tray and was about to return it to the kitchen when fingers tapped upon the door of her bedroom. She went through to open the door and Berthe was standing there, darkly severe, with the *châtelaine* rattling at the waist of her dress. 'You are to see the child,' she said at once. 'He has been bathed and put to bed, but he is still awake and M'sieur Paul has given orders that you are to present yourself to the young master.'

Margo couldn't suppress a slight smile. It sounded so old-fashioned, really, to hear a little boy referred to in such a way. To the Van Arden children she had been Margo, and they had been Polly and Junior to her, and she felt a slight sense of restriction, almost of shyness, as she went with Berthe to the lower landing, where the carpeting was thick under foot and the panels of the walls gilded and painted in the eighteenth-century style, and there was a feeling of luxury after the austerity of the upper rooms and corridors.

. As they made their way to the nursery suite Berthe indicated a pair of high double doors with rosewood

67

panels and crystal handles. 'That is the suite of the child's mother,' she said quietly. 'It was the suite she shared with her husband, and you would gasp at its beauty. But it might as well be the cell of a novice now. The poor thing takes no heed of the furnishings, and the cupboards full of clothes – so many shoes to fit her small feet, but she will never wear them again, to run skimming down the stairs to meet him when he came in from riding or cruising on the lake.'

As Berthe paused in front of the doors of the nursery suite she gave Margo almost a knowing look. 'There were many girls in his life. He was so gay – an Adonis. But she loved him. Even when he laughed at her timidity she only smiled. It took courage for her to have his child, and to go with him in that speed boat, but she went. Now there is no more courage left. He is *outre mer*, gone with his *gaieté de coeur*, and all that is left is this slip of a child. See you!'

She flung open the door and they were in the nursery, where a dim light shone beside the bed . . . a narrow white bed for a little boy, whose enormous eyes stared at Margo as she approached to look at him and to smile, and catch her breath. She had known instinctively that he would have Michel's eyes, deep and seductive as velvet, fringed by thick lashes and set in a pale olive, delicate young face. His gaze was solemn and inquiring, and every bit of woman in her wanted to grab him and hug him, and impart to him the affection for him born out of her love for his father.

'Hullo, Desi,' she said, taking a seat on the side of his bed, unaware that the muted lamplight shone on her hair and made it seem softly alive, like an aureole. 'I have come to be your governess and I do hope we are going to be good friends. Do you think we might be?'

A tiny considering frown drew his eyebrows together, and he glanced at Berthe, who stood at the foot of the bed, as if to reassure himself that the stranger had a right to be here, close to him on his bed. 'Céleste said my governess would be old and fat and I was to tell Uncle Paul that I didn't wish for her to stay. You are not old, *mademoiselle*.' His great eyes checked her over in her pale, slim-fitting dress. 'Nor are you so very fat. Are you sure you are my governess?'

'Perfectly sure, *mon enfant*.' She smiled and for the first time in this house she let a little joyous light shine in her eyes. 'My name is Margo and I'm from England. We are going to learn my language together, little by little, and I have brought with me some books by a lady called Beatrix Potter which you are going to love. Do you like animals, Desi? Do you have a pet?'

'A pet?' he murmured after her. 'That is a puppy, eh?'

'Yes, or rabbit or kitten. Do you have one of those?'

He shook his head, while Berthe lowered her voice and said quietly to Margo: 'His mother – there was an accident with a tortoise which M'sieur Paul gave him. The young *madame* had to avoid it with the wheels of her chair, one day when he took it to her room, and she was thrown out. Made hysterical but not hurt – you understand?'

Margo nodded, and felt again a longing to show Desi the gay, robust affection a child was entitled to have, especially at the age of four.

'Well, I expect there are quite a few wild creatures about the island and you and I, Desi, can go for walks and study their habits. I love birds, don't you?'

'They are not allowed on the vines,' he said, with a little touch of the family hauteur. 'They peck the grapes and Uncle Paul gets in a fury. They are kept off by the windmill at the top of the terraces. It revolves all the time like the big wings of eagles and the other smaller birds, the ones that feed on the grapes, they are kept off.'

'Well, this seems reasonable,' she said. 'Better than trapping them. Was it your uncle's idea to have the windmill put there?'

Desi nodded, and then gave a big yawn. 'I am sleepy, *mademoiselle*. We played ball, Céleste and I. She is the prettiest *jeune fille* in all the world. Uncle Paul calls her that. She likes him, and her eyes sparkle like big berries with the sun on them when she talks to him.'

'I have met Céleste, and she is very pretty. I hope you don't mind, Desi, that I am to take her place?'

'You are going to give me lessons.' He frowned again. 'I really prefer to play, but I am glad you are not old. Your hair sort of glows, like the Madonna.'

It was such a sweet, such an unexpected thing to hear from a child that Margo's throat tightened with a painful pleasure. Yes, this offspring of Michel was already a solemn little charmer, and she just had to kiss him. She just had to feel that soft olive cheek against hers. She bent her head and brushed her lips across his cheek. He submitted to the caress, but his eyes stared into hers with a sort of amazement.

'It is a goodnight kiss, Desi,' she smiled. 'A *bonsoir* salute to wish you good dreams.'

'I see.' His young face wore such an old-fashioned look, as if already a precocious young mind was blossoming ahead of his delicate, fine-boned body. 'It was pleasant, *mademoiselle*. Your lips curve, like the petals off the roses in the walled garden.'

'Young man,' she laughed unsteadily, 'you really are like your father, aren't you?'

But his heavy eyelids were closing his eyes and he didn't really hear what she said. But Berthe had heard and when they left the room and after she had carefully closed the door she gave Margo a sharp look. 'Did you know him, *mademoiselle*?'

'Did I know whom?' Margo's thoughts were centred on

the child, now asleep, the little lamp still glimmering beside his bed – as if he might be nervous of the darkness.

'The father of the boy in there! You said—'

'I – I was thinking of what you had told me – that he was an Adonis.' Margo felt the nervous stirring of her pulse as she realized that she had spoken like an intimate of Michel Cassalis. If the staff got wind of this they would soon start to talk and when the gossip reached the ears of Madame she would start asking awkward questions.

'It looks as if M'sieur Michel has passed on his charming ways to his son.' Margo looked directly at Berthe, as if she had not a thing to hide. 'I mean, Desi hardly takes after his uncle. He isn't a man to shell out many compliments, is he?'

'M'sieur Paul has more sense than to fill the heads of women with a lot of nonsense.' With a rattling of her keys Berthe went off on her round of the chateau, to lock up, no doubt, and ensure that no one had left a cigarette or a cigar burning. As Margo remembered that fallen cigar in the den a film of sweat broke over her skin, and she hurried to her suite and shut the tall door with a hunted feeling.

Now that she had met Desi, had spoken with him and kissed his young face, she didn't wish to be sent away. The boy needed her, to give him the sense of stability which Céleste, wrapped in her adolescent dreams of being loved by a tyrant, could not supply. She could give him the love which her association with his father had not fulfilled. She could win his trust, and perhaps in a while he would love her in return.

Still feeling that guilty, uncomfortable sense of warmth she went to her bathroom and took a shower. A little later, clad coolly in a nylon nightdress, she slipped into her canopied bed and lay there in the darkness, listening

71

to the sounds that were so much a part of the grounds and the lake surrounding the chateau, but which were strange to her on this her first night at Satancourt.

CHAPTER FIVE

MARGO awoke slowly to a sound she could not identify for several moments, then she realized that it came from beyond her balcony windows and was rhythmic and not really disturbing, except to a stranger in the house.

She threw aside the bedcovers and ran across the rugs to the balcony. She went outside into a shaft of sunlight across the iron and the creepers, whose flowers were unlocking in the warmth.

Across their heads, where the vine terraces rose darkly green to meet the sky, the sails of the windmill were turning, great white wings that scared away the birds from the precious ripening grapes that in the fullness of time would be crushed to make the chateau wine.

She stood there bemused by the scene, a slim figure in soft shapeless nylon, her hair in a dark red cloud about her shoulders. Sleep had fled from her eyes and the strange beauty of the scene was reflected in them. She was glad that her rooms faced the terraces and not the lake. It would have been hard to bear, to rise each morning at Satancourt and see that shining bed of death, where the willows wept.

The sound of the windmill drifted to her and she supposed that Paul Cassalis was already out among his vines, checking them over for signs of parasites, studying them as they grew and sweetened and promised him a good harvest. It would have to be a good one, for he was not a man to tolerate less than the best from his cherished, nourished, famous vines.

She returned to her room and prepared to face the day ahead of her. She took one of her starched fawn-coloured uniforms from its hanger and stepped into it, zipping the front to the small white collar. Then she combed her hair and neatly knotted it at her nape, and pinned on the cap that was to impress upon her, as well as members of the family, that she was here to do her duty and not to look decorative.

The mirror gave back her reflection and she couldn't suppress a slight smile. Well, the uniform fitted nicely, and only a mob-cap would have concealed the fact that she had, as Madame Cassalis had put it, hair like a Jezebel.

She wound her wristwatch, left her room as neat as a pin, and made her way downstairs. A sound of activity came from the direction of the kitchen, but the main body of the chateau was quiet and she guessed that members of the family, apart from the head of it, did not rise this early for breakfast. She decided to have a look round and after opening a few doors that led into closets and broom cupboards, not to mention a fragrant little flower room, she eventually found the door that led into the courtyard and she proceeded along a covered way, gauzy with overnight webs and dew, until she reached the great tiled court, where the ancient walls were thick with creepers, spangled by the knotty branches of wistaria, and redolent of damp stone and tumbling geraniums.

She took a deep breath of the fresh air, and saw some geese grubbing about near a stone stable, with tethering rings in the wall, and a pile of aubergines bronzing in the sun. She smelled straw and heard the stamp of horses, and the sound was tempting. She had learned to ride while in America and hoped that she would be allowed to ride while she was here.

She walked under an archway and found herself on a paved path that led in the direction of the lake. She hesitated, and then decided that she must face it, must grow used to the wide vista of water upon which a speeding boat had exploded, filling the air with flame and oil, while a scream echoed, as the bird calls echoed.

The path stretched ahead of her and as the wind across the water caught at her cap and threatened to blow it off her head, she removed the pin and carried the cap in her hand. The wind across her brow was like the stroke of a velvet paw, cool without being cold, and so refreshing. Lovely, deceptive lake, slumbering in the morning sun, hiding its secrets behind a smile, like a sensuous woman. She stood still among the willows and was watching the dark wings of birds etching patterns against the sky when her ears caught the sound of hoofbeats.

She swiftly turned her head in the direction of the sound, coming not from the chateau but from the haze that still hung over the path that traversed the distance of the lake. The horse and rider came out of the web of mist, formed by the dew as the sun drew it out of the tall grass, and she saw the satin gleam of the black horse, and tall in the saddle the figure of Paul Cassalis, the whiteness of his shirt making his skin seem like living teak, the material stretched taut across his wide, strong shoulders.

'*Bonjour, mademoiselle!*' He brought the animal to a halt only a short breath away from her slim, uniformed figure. He slitted his eyes against the bright reflected light from the lake and this gave to their grey-cobalt an even more piercing quality, like fine steel sliding over her and stripping away all outer clothing to her white body itself. The look, and the memory of their embrace of the night before, made it impossible for Margo to answer him. All she could do was stand there and wish there had been time for her to scamble off the path before they met like this, in this lonely place.

He leaned from the saddle and the very tip of his whip whispered across her shoulder. 'Have you lost your tongue, Miss Jones? Last night you had plenty to say and no fear of saying it. Have I startled you, coming upon you so suddenly?'

'Yes.' The truth had its way with her as always, especially in his company. 'I took it for granted you were up on the terraces attending to your vines.'

'I have been up there,' he said. 'There is a break in this path which leads to them, but now I am on my way back to the chateau for my breakfast. I am entitled to that, eh?'

She caught the glimmer of amusement in his eyes, and then he tilted back his head and the wind stirred his heavy black hair. There were lines etched deep beside his mouth, those of authority and the various anxieties of the *vigneron*, but there wasn't a streak of grey in his hair. There was a satanic kind of attraction about the man, and here by the lake, which seemed to whisper seductively where the reeds waved slim and green, she could imagine that doomed and secret affair between him and the young maid to Madame Cassalis.

Had they met here, on this path, in the dark instead of in the daylight?

'You are very much the nursemaid this morninng,' he said, and the word he used made all her nerves tighten. What had he in mind – another seduction of a girl working here on her own, far from her family, and foolish enough to believe he would make her his wife?

'Madame Cassalis wished me to wear uniform, though at my other post I wore ordinary clothing.' Margo spoke very formally, determined to let him know that she was here to work and not to play – least of all with him.

'We aren't ogres here, *mademoiselle*. If you don't wish to wear a uniform then you will not be forced into one. Maman is slightly old-fashioned, that is all—'

'I don't mind,' Margo broke in. 'Desi will take more notice of what I say, and he won't make the mistake of regarding me as – as a member of your family.'

'It would never do for such a mistake to be made, eh?' And in that instant his hand must have tightened on the

76

rein of the horse, for abruptly the long legs shifted their position and Margo found herself forced back against the edge of the lake. The heel of her shoe slipped on some wet weeds and to save herself she had to go forward again, and the mettlesome black jingled his harness and was made nervous by her outflung hand. He reared and for a moment the vicious hooves waved in her face.

'Out of the way!' Paul ordered, and she ran past the reared-up horse, ran on along the path in the direction of the chateau. Her heart was thumping, and she wanted to make it to the entrance before he caught up with her. She heard the hooves pounding behind her and it was as if she were being deliberately chased. When she reached the archway that led into the courtyard she flung round and gave Paul Cassalis a stormy look. He saluted her with his whip, mockingly, and as he cantered past her he called out:

'Nervous women and horses don't mix. Learn to control your nerves, Miss Jones, or you will be in trouble the next time we meet.'

'In future,' she said angrily, 'I shall do my best to avoid running into you. I have no wish to be trampled on, or to end up in the lake.'

'Can't you swim?' he drawled, and rode on past her in the direction of the stables, and she heard a squawk as a white goose fluttered out of his path. She also heard him laugh, as if the symbolism was vastly amusing to him.

Gritting her teeth and hating his male arrogance, Margo entered the hall of the chateau and found a mirror so she could smooth her hair and pin on her cap. Her ruffled feelings weren't so easily smoothed, and looking into her own reflected eyes she saw how they burned with temper – and with excitement.

She turned away from the mirror, for she knew she had glimpsed her secret self, a person who was wholly alive again, vibrant and tingling in every nerve of her body.

That was why she had reacted so swiftly to every ripple and breath of that arrogant body upon the saddle of that equally dangerous horse. A flame had been lit, and much as she hated it, she couldn't stamp it out because it was a flame of the senses, and as some of the heat licked across her cheekbones she covered them with her hands and was standing thus when one of the maids came into the hall with a duster in her hand.

'*Bonjour, mademoiselle.*' The girl offered a smile even as she stared rather curiously at the English Miss, standing there holding her face as if she had the toothache. 'You are feeling quite all right?'

'Oh – yes, thank you.' Margo pulled herself together. 'I was just wondering where to go for my breakfast. I have three choices and I am bound to pick on the wrong one. Do I eat in the kitchen, the nursery, or the dining-room? Can you tell me?'

The young maid shook her head, and then hastened away to her dusting as Berthe appeared, the rattling of her keys a forewarning to any of the servants who happened to be loitering about. With a quick smile of relief Margo turned to her. The housekeeper would know, surely, what the protocol was regarding breakfast, and Margo was beginning to feel quite a need for bacon and egg, rounded off with toast and marmalade. It must have been all that fresh air from the lake!

'The staff have eaten,' said Berthe, shortly. 'M'sieur Hercule is now preparing breakfast for the family, and I understand that you are to join them for meals. If you will come this way, Miss Jones, I will show you the break-fast patio. Madame alone has breakfast in her room, and during this time she also writes her letters.'

'What of – Maxine?' Margo was beginning to have the odd feeling that Michel's widow was like a ghost at the chateau, an unseen presence whom everyone seemed to wish to forget.

'She has only coffee and eats very poorly. The poor thing spends the fine days on her veranda, reading a little, and remembering a lot.'

'And Desi?'

'It is still too early for the child to be aroused, and I understand that you will attend from now on to the matter of his bath and his meals. After M'sieur Paul has eaten and left for his work, you may bring the child to the patio for his milk and his egg. It is for you to decide, Miss Jones. You are now in charge of his welfare.'

This sounded very promising, but Margo wasn't counting her chicks until they were out of the shell. Somehow she couldn't imagine a regime of total freedom, with no interference from Madame Cassalis. The child was her grandson and she would ensure that the English governess did not instil into him any ideas contrary to her own. The first signs of them would be firmly checked, Margo was certain of that.

Berthe paused and indicated a small flight of twisting stairs, built it seemed in the very wall of the chateau. 'They lead to the patio,' she said, 'which is more or less a roof garden over the old wine pressing room. When up-to-date equipment was installed in the windmill, this part of the chateau would have fallen into disuse if M'sieur Paul had not seen a way to make it useful. There are the stairs, of course, but he likes it up there—'

'You mean he'll be there – now?' Margo exclaimed. Somehow she had hoped he would rush through his coffee and rolls and be off.

'Where else would he be? A man his size does not live on the air.' Berthe looked at Margo as if she were a fool. 'If you will tell me now what you wish for breakfast, I will see that Lucille brings it to you as soon as possible.'

For a wild moment Margo was tempted to say that she didn't require breakfast after all, and then her stomach, not to mention her spirit, reasserted their claims, and she gave her order. 'I hope it's all right for me to have an English breakfast, Berthe? But if coffee and *croissants* are the order of the day—?'

'M'sieur thinks nothing of asking for kidneys, or sliced truffles, so let it not bother you that you require a plate of cooked food first thing in the morning.' Berthe looked at Margo as if she were dealing with a young woman of uncivilized habits. Men were different. Men had what they fancied, when the fancy for it took them. That was the understood way of life, and the acceptance of this, and the wariness of the girl from England, were reflected in the Gallic dark eyes of Berthe.

'You are kind, thank you,' said Margo, and she felt sure that underneath the severe exterior there lurked a certain kindness of heart. But Berthe was a busy woman; the keys of the chateau were in her hands and she had many responsibilities. Margo could not blame her if she had little time to spare for a new arrival, and with a little sigh, a quickening of apprehension through her veins, Margo mounted the spiral stairs and stepped out on to the roof patio.

She heard voices at once, and caught the girlish laughter of Céleste. The girl was seated with Paul at a circular cane table, her seal-brown hair tailed in a ribbon of red, very young and pretty in contrast to his virile figure. She was nibbling toast while he was busily eating from a plate of tomatoes, sausages and egg.

Margo saw all this in a flash, and she also felt an intruder as she approached the table, the starchy rustle of her uniform catching the attention of Céleste, who turned her head swiftly, and lost her smile with equal swiftness.

'Oh – did you want something, Miss Jones?' She spoke in such an officious young voice that Margo felt like giving her a smart answer.

Paul glanced up from his food lazily, and a burst of sun

through the plumbago made his hair very black and his shirt very white. There were no half-shades about Paul Cassalis. He was like a Rodin sculpture, hard as rock, and yet with a skin like warm brandy.

'Miss Jones has come to have her breakfast,' he said, a tremor of secret laughter in his voice. 'Do come to the table, *mademoiselle*, and while you await your food do pour yourself a cup of coffee from the pot. It was brought boiling to the table and the sun has kept it hot. What do you think of our weather? *Le bon protecteur* is good to us. If this continues then the wine will be full of sparkle, gaiety – a true champagne.'

Margo sat down in one of the cane chairs, and as she picked up the coffee pot a little gold spider ran across the white cloth. She and Paul saw it at the same instant and their eyes met. 'A money spider, *m'sieur*.'

'Yes, *mademoiselle*, but I am not only concerned to make my fortune.'

'Are you not?' She stirred cream into her coffee. 'You seem very ambitious to me.'

'My ambitions are various, and I wonder, *mademoiselle*, what yours are under that crisp and efficient exterior? I could make several guesses, but you are something of a sphinx and I would not like to say that I could guess your secret.'

The word jarred on her and once again she wondered if he knew that in days gone by she had been intoxicated by the charm of his brother. It was a relief when Céleste broke in eagerly on the conversation. 'Can you guess, Paul, what my ambition is?'

'Yes, little one.' His tone of voice was all at once indulgent.

'Can you really?' She tossed her head and her tail of hair gave a flirt. 'Then I am not a sphinx?'

'With your *jeunesse, petite*, you are clear as a wine glass before one pours into it the wine of kisses and tears.'

'Meaning I'm a kid!' Céleste exclaimed. 'Meaning I haven't been around and acquired the ability of Miss Jones to hide her feelings. I hope I am married by the time I reach her age.'

'I am not Methuselah's aunt,' Margo said drily.

'But all the same you are attractive enough to be married.' Céleste was staring at her. 'It is all very well for women who have no sex appeal to take up a career, but you look quite sexy to me. I am sure Paul would agree. You are a man, Paul. What do you say? Do you consider that Miss Jones is wasting herself as a child's *bonne*?'

His eyes flicked Margo's face, which was as cool and controlled as she could make it in the circumstances. Inwardly she was filled with the urge to jump to her feet and run away from these two, who seemed to have her at their mercy, up here on the roof of the old wine-pressing room, changed into a patio by the addition of giant pots filled with the type of plants that grew abundantly in the hot sunshine. With ornamental iron at the edges of the circular roof, in case someone should go too near the edge and lose their balance. With the sound of birds in the air, perhaps hawk-sparrows hunting prey in the scarves of ivy mantling the turrets just across the slim bridge of stone joining the cluster of roofs together.

Overhead the sky was blue and growing hot, and far below them the lake was silvery and cool.

'The motives of Miss Jones in coming to work here are not for you to delve into.' Paul spoke to Céleste, but he was still looking at Margo with that tiny mocking gleam in his eyes, as if to warn her that he would do as he pleased; delve whenever he felt inclined, and make her respond to him if he so wished.

She glared at him and her hand tensed on the table. If he should ever touch her again she would slap him across that brown, arrogant face and not count the cost.

Then came footsteps, and it was the maid Lucille

bringing her breakfast, crisp bacon and eggs perfectly fried so the yolks were intact under a filmy skin. Toast and marmalade, and ripe apricots.

'You are going to eat all that?' Céleste exclaimed.

'I'm afraid I always eat well,' said Margo, and she flicked a look across Paul's face. 'But I promise to earn my keep. I understand, *m'sieur*, that I am to be in complete charge of your nephew. I hope this means I can take him on walks about the island? He seemed a trifle pale to me, as if he is kept confined to the chateau a lot of the time.'

'I used to take him out,' said Céleste. 'I have been his companion.'

'Yes,' said Paul, 'but you had a habit of taking him to the pavilion beside the lake, where you would read those romantic stories while the child was kept sleepy and quiet with too much chocolate. That is why I had Maman interview for an English *bonne*. They have fresh air ideas and they don't spoil a boy with too much petting.'

'You can be so cutting, like a knife.' Céleste pouted her youthful red mouth at him, more in invitation than rebuke. 'I suppose you want him to grow up like you, with a heart of stone?'

'At least with a sense of discipline, *ma fille*. You were spoiled yourself as a child, whereas Miss Jones has been a working girl from an early age. I think she knows that I want Desi to have a sense of responsibility and to have an awareness that it's good for the soul, as well as the body, to toil for one's bread.'

'What a bore, Paul! The only people who work are those who have to, and tyrants like yourself who think everything will go wrong unless their eagle eye is forever on the watch.' Céleste gave him an impudent smile and lolled in her chair like a kitten in the sun. 'Maxine wishes me to attend the Swiss finishing school where she went herself, but I like to be here with – my sister. I am really necessary to her now that Papa has married again and taken for a wife that *midinette* little older than dear Maxine herself. It is – immature of him!'

'It is loneliness, Céleste. A man's kind of loneliness, and perhaps love.'

'Love?' She looked scornful. 'You don't believe in it! You said once to Raoul that it was the emotion best left to women and avoided by men. You said that men should be ruled by the brain and not by the body—'

'I had been sampling wine that day with Raoul d'Arcy, if I remember correctly. You had no place to be listening to such a conversation. Were you hiding?'

'Yes, in the *chai* among the wine casks.' She giggled at the frown on his face. 'I was sixteen then, a child, and I thought it would be fun to eavesdrop on you and Raoul, who is so very Parisian even when he comes to Satancourt. I hoped he would have some naughty stories to tell you, but it was even better when he began to talk about – women. He must have had dozens of affairs.'

'Raoul is a talker and fond of exaggerating.' Paul climbed to his feet, as if suddenly he wanted an end to the conversation. 'It is time for me to go and rattle my sabre over my poor downtrodden workers. Are you coming down with me to say *bonjour* to your sister, or are you staying to keep Miss Jones company while she finishes her breakfast?'

'I will come with you.' Céleste was upon her feet in an instant and she reached out to hold his arm, to feel the warmth and hardness of him close to her. Yes, thought Margo, the girl was infatuated with his maleness, of having to tilt back her head on her slim neck to look at him to see in his face the danger of the fully emancipated and experienced man.

'We will leave you, Miss Jones,' he said. 'Have a good day and feel free to take Desi out into the fresh air, only be careful of the lake. Parts of it are very deep and we should not wish for another accident.'

Margo watched him walk away with Céleste, and as they disappeared down the steps to the interior of the chateau she gave a little shiver. He had seemed to show little emotion as he spoke, yet she had seen the shadow in his eyes, the dulling over of the piercing eyes, as if for an instant the sun over the day had died for him. Was his sorrow for Michel, who had not once mentioned him during those two months at Cannes? Or was he remembering the girl ... young, pretty and foolish ... who had ended in the lake?

After finishing her food, Margo strolled to the iron-grilled parapet and let her eyes feast on the clustering turrets, tawny coloured with black slated conical roofs, adding such a picturesque air to the chateau. The cloaks of ivy were densely green, so closely attached to the walls that the effect was one of a mantle of green velvet.

This was what Paul Cassalis loved above all ... and this was what Desi must be taught to love. The *esprit de famille*. Duty before personal love of a woman.

And who, she wondered, as she made for the steps that spiralled down into the heart of the chateau, was Raoul d'Arcy?

The nursery suite when she reached it was bright with sunshine. Desi was out of his bed, half out of his pyjamas and playing with a set of coloured soldiers on the floor. He glanced up in his solemn way when she entered. '*Bonjour*, Desi.' She smiled at him and knelt down on a woolly rug go take a look at his toys. They were beautifully carved out of wood and painted with the same amount of charming care. 'I say, these are grand. And real fur hats for your hussars! You are a lucky chap.'

She spoke in English, testing his ability so far with her language. For a moment more he studied her, taking in her uniform and the cap that was crisp against the copper of her hair.

'*J'aime les* soldiers.' He knew that word. '*Mon oncle*

Raoul, he make them.'

Ah, that name again! She was beginning to have the feeling that the sophisticated Raoul from Paris was a man of talent as well as charm. She picked up one of the soldiers, about four inches high and made with such exactitude that only a child of sensitive appreciation should own them.

'And have you a fort to go with them, Desi?' She reverted to French, and at once he broke into a smile and ran to a cupboard set deep in a wall of the room. He flung open the door and revealed the shelves of toys; not the cheap kind that could be broken and forgotten, but good toys, well made, and made to last. He scrambled about in the bottom of the cupboard and emerged with the fort in his arms. As he brought it to Margo with an air of triumph, she caught her breath and was irresistibly reminded of Michel buying all the mimosa she had for sale and marching off with it in his arms. When she had arrived home from work she had found her room filled with it. He had bribed the landlady to let him into her lodging, and he had left perfume with the flowers, from Chanel, and a card bearing the words:

'Dary Rose *que j'adore*!' She had smiled, she remembered, and buried her face in the flowers. He always called her a rose because he said she had thorns a yard long whenever he became too much the ardent lover.

'Look, *mademoiselle*.' Desi was tugging at her arm, urging her to awake from her reverie and take notice of what he had to show her. 'See, I have cannons and little cannonballs, and these soldiers here, they have muskets and these are on horseback and they are the cavalry. They batter down the gates, you see, after much fighting, and they charge into the fort. Is it not exciting?'

'It is an exciting game,' she agreed, and looked at his tousled dark hair and his eager eyes and all her doubts melted away. In his way Michel had loved her, and already his small son was stealing away her heart.

'We will play,' he announced. 'I shall be Napoleon, of course, and you will be my enemy.'

'Darling,' she laughed, 'I hope to be your friend.'

They played for about half an hour, then she insisted that he be popped in the bath with his rubber dolphin while she rang for his milk, egg and fruit.

'Are you going to give me lessons?' he asked, as he splashed the dolphin among the bubbles and enjoyed making everything in sight as wet as possible.

Margo had swathed herself in a big white nursery overall and was glad of it. 'I thought we'd get acquainted, *mon ami*. The gardens of the chateau are a wonderful playground, filled with trees and plants, and we will take a ramble among them and I shall tell you their names in English. *D'accord, beau sabreur?*'

'*En effet*. I am much happy, *mademoiselle*, that you have come to be my governess. You are *jolie femme*,' and then he started to giggle, 'but you look so funny in the big overall!'

She swooped on him and was tickling him in the water when Berthe entered with a rustle and a rattle, a tray in her hands. She stared at the scene, and tut-tutted at the amount of water over the tiled floor. 'I see, Miss Jones, that you are making yourself busy, but I would point out that it is not the usual practice to let the child behave like a little bear. You must exert the discipline, or my girls will spend half the morning mopping up this bathroom and putting away his toys.'

Margo glanced up, grinning, her cap askew, and her eyes densely blue. 'I shall see to the bathroom and the nursery, Berthe. You need not worry that we will leave the place like a bear-garden. After Desi has had his breakfast we are going for a walk. The garden is as big as a jungle and we have so much to discover together—'

'What of his lessons, Miss Jones? You are aware that

you were not hired just to – to amuse the boy?'

'If I amuse him, Berthe, then all to the good.' She smiled and enveloped the boy in a large bath towel. 'We have to become accustomed to each other, eh, *mon petit*? And look at the sun! It is too lovely a day for the blackboard and the chalk.'

Grumbling to herself about the inadvisability of hiring a member of the mad British race to conduct the education of a French child, Berthe took the tray into the nursery. Desi looked at Margo, and she looked at him, and their eyes spoke a humorous language of their own, long forgotten by poor Berthe with all her household duties.

It was while he was finishing his apricots that Margo broached a delicate subject, difficult to mention and yet unavoidable. 'Your *maman*, Desi? Do you go in the mornings to wish her a good day?'

He licked juice from his lips and turned his empty eggshell upside down so he could break it with his spoon. '*Non.*' He shook his dark head. 'Maman likes to be alone in the mornings. Sometimes I go to see her in the afternoons, but not if she is feeling low. She suffers.' They were such adult and poignant words to hear from a child. 'I have to be quiet, you see, and not disturb her. She was with Papa when he was drowned, and she grieves for him.'

And in that instant, as Margo gazed at the downbent head of her young and rather lonely little pupil, there rushed over her a feeling of impatience with Maxine. Of course she had suffered. What more heartbreaking than to lose a young husband? But there was Desi to consider. She had something very precious of Michel to live for, yet he was kept out of her way and she was allowed by Madame Cassalis and by Paul to mope in her room and dwell on the past instead of looking forward to the future.

Margo resolved that something must be done to awake Maxine's interest in her son, but right now she and Desi had a wild and rambling garden to explore, so unexpected, and not at all like those formal French gardens on the Côte d'Azur, with their statuary and their formalized flower beds and exquisite garden pools.

She placed the empty cup and plates on the tray, made certain the nursery suite was tidy, and herself also, and she and Desi made their way along the quiet corridor, past the elegant doors of Maxine's suite, and down the stairs. They were halfway down when they met Yvonne Dalbert, notebook in hand, neat as a pin with not a dark hair out of place, and obviously on her way to Madame's suite.

She flicked her eyes over Margo's uniform and a tiny gleam of satisfaction seemed to lighten her sallow countenance for a moment. To see Margo looking like a member of the staff obviously made up a little for not seeing her ignominiously dismissed from the chateau. Then she glanced at Desi and said coldly: 'You should have informed Miss Jones that you only wear your blue shirts on a Sunday. The white shirts are for every day.'

'Desi did tell me,' Margo broke in, 'but I felt that white was a little too formal on such a bright day – in fact I am going to ask Madame if some more coloured shirts can be added to his wardrobe. Children so love bright colours.'

'Desi is not *children*,' snapped Yvonne, discarding all pretence at amiability. 'He is the grandson of Madame Cassalis and he is to look the young gentleman at all times. No doubt you are accustomed to hooligans—'

'No, *mademoiselle*,' Margo cut in, 'nor am I accustomed to your type of insolence, usually associated with the insecure.'

Colour flared across the sallow face, and before Yvonne Dalbert could give voice to the words trembling on her lips, Margo grabbed Desi's hand and hurried him down the stairs to the hall. They sped across to the covered way that led out to the courtyard, but when they were almost there he came to a halt and tugged free of her hand. He ran into the adjacent flower room, dived under the bench where the flowers were cut for arranging in the tall vases, and emerged with a big coloured ball.

'I keep it there for convenience,' he panted. 'If Berthe should see it she would throw it in the incinerator, but Jules, who brings in the flowers, he lets me keep it there. Is it not a splendid playball?'

'Magnificent. And who bought you that?' She caught the ball in her arms as he tossed it to her. 'Shall I make a guess?'

He nodded, made a dart at a lizard and almost caught it by the tail, which just flickered out of his hand in time. 'It would have come away anyway,' he said. 'Lizards are clever. They can escape just by unlocking their tails – did you know that, *mademoiselle*?'

'I do now,' she smiled. 'I bet your Uncle Raoul bought you the ball?'

'Wrong!' He made a dart at the fountain, jumped up the steps and clapped his hands in the sprays of water. 'It was Uncle Paul and I should think you would know that he would give me such a present. He says I am to learn how to kick it and to grow big like him. I think it will take me some time to grow big. Grand'mère says I am like my father. He was *élégant*, I think, but I should prefer to be fearsome like Uncle Paul. Jules says he is the devil at times, but I have never seen his tail, unless he unlocks it like the lizard. Do you think he does, *mademoiselle*?'

'I very much doubt it, *mon petit*.' She quickly suppressed a smile. 'Now shall we go for that walk under the trees? It will be cooler than being here in the courtyard.'

He acquiesced and they went further into the garden, where the trees met overhead and great sprays of flowers scented the green cloisters. 'Have you a garden such as this at your home in England?' Desi glanced up at her as he strolled alongside her with his hands in the pockets of his short pants. Margo still carried the coloured ball, for when they reached a shady clearing they could play with it out of range of the fine old windows for which Berthe obviously feared.

'We had a cottage garden when I was your age, Desi, but the dust from the coalmines showered the petals of the flowers and there were always smuts on them. We lived in the shadow of a great mountain made up of coal dust and it used to shut out the sun so the flowers never grew as big as these in your garden.'

'It sounds a little – sad,' he said, with that precocious sensitivity which made him seem unchildlike at times. 'Did you have brothers and sisters?'

'Yes, so things weren't too bad. We had each other to play with and we knew no other world, so we thought ours was the only world. In fact, at times, it was rather beautiful in a strange way. We would listen to the miners singing their songs as they trudged home from their work, and to this day I can remember those deep fine voices and the wonderful sound of the music. Do you like music, Desi?'

He nodded. 'I like it when the grape-pickers sing their songs,' he said. 'They are so gay, and Uncle Paul he sings with them—'

'Paul does?' It was so amazing that she forgot to tag on the correct appellation, and then as she thought of those broad shoulders and that deep chest she realized that it wasn't so amazing that he liked to sing; many of the miners had been built along the same rugged lines and their voices had been superb. She could only suppose that after his sardonic treatment of herself she wanted to believe only dark things about him and had a disinclination to envisage him swinging basket loads of grapes on to the carts while he laughed and sang with his wine workers. Yet the image was vivid . . . almost intolerably so.

'The wine terraces are very beautiful,' she said. 'I never realized until I came here that the vines were so green. Do you look forward to picking grapes when you are bigger, Desi?'

'I go with Uncle Paul to pick the first of the harvest,' he said importantly. 'We taste them together to see that they are sweet and ready for the making of the wine. I have tasted wine also. My uncle says I am to be a true *vigneron* like he is.'

Margo frowned slightly, for it didn't seem right to her that a small boy should be given wine. Desi grinned up at her. 'It was only a very tiny glass, *mademoiselle*, to baptize me, Uncle Paul said.'

'He would,' she murmured and when Desi cocked his head in an old-fashioned way, she realized that these asides were being picked up by his busy little brain and might be repeated when he found himself alone with that uncle of his. Suddenly Desi darted from her side and ran to a tree where the ground underneath was bare of the flowers and leaf that grew so abundantly under the other trees.

'This is *trufflère!*' he said excitedly, and he began to dig at the soil with his hands, like a puppy scrabbling for a bone, and Margo was about to protest that he would get the dirt all over his shirt and pants when he tore a dark object from the ground, wrinkled like a dried fruit and big as Desi's hand.

'See!' He held it out with a look of rapture. 'Such a *bonne femme* of a truffle and in the ground a long time. I shall give it to Maman for her dinner – the truffle is good for people, yes, and it has magic in it.'

'How did you know it was there?' Fascinated, Margo knelt beside him and gazed at the odd-looking fruit of the ground that was reputed to be so delicious. She could not recall what the truffle had tasted like which she had shared with Michel; she had been too beguiled by the man to care or know what she was eating.

'Because of the bare ground, *mademoiselle*. They are greedy, are truffles, and they like to grow by themselves. Uncle Paul says they kill the herbs and flowers that dare to share their bed.'

'Really?' Gazing at Desi with the truffle held in his hands as if it were a rose she realized why he had such an old-fashioned head on his young shoulders. *Mon oncle* was his oracle, passing on to the boy all his own knowledge of the French soil, and the Gallic soul. Desi could kick balls and have soldiers, by all means, but there had been no teddy bears in his cupboard. He was to learn early to be a man, and he was being trained to emulate the hard, forthright Paul, steeped in the pagan rites of wine culture and arrogantly proud of the land which the violent past had yielded into Cassalis hands, never to leave them while men like Paul were born, and shaped to his image, his actions, and his desires.

Margo spent all the morning with Desi, and they had lunch with Céleste on the roof garden. Desi still had the truffle with him and it reposed beside his plate as he ate his food and Céleste wrinkled her nose and asked him what he intended doing with it.

'It is for Maman,' he replied. 'I shall give it to M'sieur Hercule and he will put it in a casserole for her. She will be pleased with me.'

'Yes, of course, little one.' Céleste shrugged her shoulders at Margo, as if to say that her sister Maxine would show little interest in the boy or his absurd truffle.

'Will it be possible for me to meet your sister today?' Margo asked. 'I think I should have a few words with her regarding Desi. She may wish—'

'Her wishes are Madame's and Paul's.' Céleste was quite emphatic. 'I am afraid my sister has withdrawn into

93

a world of her own — 'you see she was heartbroken when Michel—' Again Céleste shrugged her shoulders, and then turned her attention to Desi, leaving Margo to mull over her words as the sun grew hot above the trees shading their table and the vine terraces in the distance took on a blue-green shimmer as of a veil over the land.

She would find a way to meet Maxine. She would go to her suite on her own initiative and try to awake her to the fact that other people were taking over her son and trying to mould him not in the likeness of his father but in that of his uncle.

Maxine had obviously adored Michel, so she must be made to care that Desi was being taught to forget the charming man who had fathered him.

A mutinous light glowed in Margo's eyes. She had loved Michel herself, and she was deeply antagonistic towards Paul. Brothers, and yet so unalike. Not only in looks but in ways. She decided that Paul was a throwback, still stamped with a Breton wildness, and not to be tamed . . . by hate or love.

CHAPTER SIX

But the days that followed were so filled with discovery for Margo, and she was kept so busy teaching her young pupil the English names of all they saw and heard about the chateau that there was little chance to carry out her plan to approach Maxine.

She caught glimpses of her on the veranda of her suite, sitting there alone in the stillness of later afternoon and seemingly unaware of the other occupants of the house; lost in her memories, which were gradually becoming more real to her than the sound of her son's voice and all the little eager things he longed to run and tell her.

It was easy enough for Margo to tell herself that she would break in on the seclusion so dear to Maxine, but when it came to the point it was not at all easy to walk in on that sad girl. Twice Margo almost did so; her hand was on the door when her resolve fled away and she felt almost afraid of meeting the eyes of Maxine, of seeing her scarred face, of saying outright that she owed it to her son to awake from her sad dreams to the reality of the present.

Margo's sensitivity recoiled from the idea of hurting someone who had already been hurt almost beyond bearing.

So, for the time being, she gave all her attention to Desi. She was ever ready to listen to his chatter, to answer his many questions, and read him stories. In the afternoons when he took his nap she was sometimes called to the sitting-room of Madame Cassalis to report on his progress. She was well aware that Madame was keeping a shrewd eye on her, but so far she seemed satisfied – apart from this matter of Margo dining with the family each evening. To do so Margo had to discard her uniform and wear one of her simple evening dresses, and more than once she had caught a chilly look in the grey eyes, and there were times when rebellion flared through Margo's veins and she longed to cry out:

'Throw open your windows, *madame*, and let in the laughter of the people outside your planned and ordered life. Your values belong to the past ... it is no longer fashionable and brave to walk head in the air rather than to be warm and human like the people in the street, those who sell from the market stalls, those who pick your grapes, and those who sew your evening gowns. Relax and be a little more human, Madame Cassalis.'

The tensions of these evenings were building up in Margo, for always Paul was present and he seemed to reap a subtle enjoyment out of her torment – she felt sure of it. He knew what relief it would have been if he had suddenly said to her: 'Take yourself off, *mademoiselle*. Go and eat on your balcony if you wish, but for the sake of heaven don't sit there looking as if this is the last meal of the condemned prisoner!'

The very words seemed to smoulder in his eyes like tiny devils, jibing at her, daring her to do something that would shake the formality of the conversation at the table, and the business talk in the *salon* after the meal where coffee and cognac were served.

Margo sat there with her coffee cup in her hand, breathing the fragrance of the cognac as it arose in the steam of the coffee. From the first evening with the family she had followed Paul's action in tipping his brandy into his cup, not because she liked the man, but because he had an appreciation of what was palatable. During the day he looked the typical *vigneron* in his open-collared shirt and breeches, but in the evenings, clad in his impeccable black and white, he was the man of the world.

He had an air of making every other man she had ever seen look callow, and to meet his eyes made Margo feel callow herself, as if she knew very little about life in comparison to him.

He stood there, where the brocade curtains were drawn open to let in the scents of the night and the glow of the new risen moon, so dark as to be an assault on the gracious furnishings of the room, as if the sudden movement of his hand might break something, or a turn of his big body send a porcelain object crashing to the floor.

As he stood there, quietly sipping his coffee, his eyes seemed to be saying a hundred mocking things ... reminding her always that she had been in his arms and for hateful, tempestuous moments he had made her forget the kisses of his brother. He didn't – couldn't know that she had cared for Michel, but he did know that he antagonized her. It was there in his eyes, the awareness of how she felt about him, and the mocking disregard of her feelings.

She knew she ought to be more amiable, because she had grown fond of Desi and it was within Paul's power to snatch from her the delight and amusement she found in his nephew's company. She felt all the time that she was being tested by him, pushed to the edge of rebellion and then coaxed back to obedience by the subtle mastery which he exerted over everyone, including his mother. Margo sensed the affection between them, but it was rarely displayed in more than a brief meeting of their eyes, or in the smile that might touch his lips and then be gone again.

It was always a relief for Margo when the lovely old clock struck the hour of ten and Madame would rise to her feet and announce that she was going to bed. She would look at Yvonne, then at Margo, and her look would coolly indicate that they were expected to follow her upstairs to their rooms.

But tonight it was only nine-thirty when she rose from her sofa and pressed a hand to her forehead. 'I have one of my headaches, Paul. This warm weather seems to bring them on, and I really must go to my room. Yvonne, I shall require you to ease the nape of my neck with a cologne massage; it really is the only remedy which brings me some relief.'

'*Oui, madame.*' Yvonne rose dutifully to her feet, and as she did so she cast a look at Margo as if to say that if her own evening was curtailed she saw no reason why the governess should have an additional half hour in the company of M'sieur Paul. She made no pretence of liking Margo, who was inclined to suspect that Madame's companion had a crush on Paul, but it wasn't to please Yvonne that Margo prepared to leave the *salon*. She had no wish to be left alone with him, and it came as a shock when he said to his mother:

'I wish Miss Jones to remain for a while so that we might discuss the progress of the boy. I hope your headache is soon cured, Maman.'

His mother paused by the door and gave him a sharp look. 'I have already quizzed Miss Jones on Desi's progress, so there is no need for you to waste your time going over the same ground, Paul. I am satisfied that Mademoiselle is doing her duties quite well.'

'Then Mademoiselle will remain to share a glass of wine with me,' he said deliberately. 'I require a little company after a long day's work and as you have a headache, Maman, I shall not detain you, or the good Yvonne, who is so necessary to you. Miss Jones, you will remain in the *salon*, if you please!'

Margo was half-way to the door when these words lashed at her and brought her up short. In that startled second a vivid image of what it might mean to be alone with Paul flashed through her mind and gave her the courage to defy him. She swung round, and as she did so the brilliant light of the French chandelier cascaded over her hair and the dark fiery gleam to it seemed a reflection of her quick temper.

'I am a little tired, *m'sieur*. I wish to go to my room.'

'You don't look at all tired, *mademoiselle*, but that is not a reflection on your labours.' He walked past her to the door and held it open for his mother and Yvonne. '*Bon soir*, ladies. I will not detain you.'

It was a firm dismissal, and after they had left the room he closed the door and stood looking at Margo, one hand casually at rest in the pocket of his dinner jacket. 'At your age, and with your vitality, you could dance till two in the morning and not feel tired,' he drawled. 'I can imagine that you are very fond of dancing. You have the legs and feet for it. There is a swift grace to you, *mademoiselle*, and the high temper of the unbroken filly.'

'Is it your intention to break me in, *m'sieur*?' She tossed her head and her hair gleamed the colour of dark fire about the pallor of her neck and the fine planing of her cheekbones. Her eyes were densely blue and filled with defiance. He must know that his behaviour would antagonize his mother and increase the hostility of her companion, and Margo made up her mind that she wasn't going to have her position put into jeopardy because he felt bored, and in the mood for a little diversion after his long day among the vines.

'I am not standing for this,' she said. 'As an employee I need the good will of your mother, not her suspicions that I am after her son. She warned me in London—'

'Warned you, *mademoiselle*?' His voice was a whisper, the merest hiss of the whip. 'Against me?'

'Against having ideas that you were – eligible.' There was an added edge of scorn to Margo's voice because of the hurt she had suffered over letting herself believe that Michel had been free to court her and make her love her. 'I don't want anyone here at the chateau to harbour the idea that I am looking for a rich husband. I am here to work.'

'An admirable ambition, Miss Jones.' He moved lazily forward and she was obliged to retreat from his advance or find herself altogether too close to his darkness, his height, and his infernal mockery. 'But tell me, for I am most intrigued, what gives you the idea that I am not eligible as a husband? I have all my limbs and faculties, as far as I know, and though I can't be called rich in these days of highway tax robbery I am in a position to support an attractive wife with a flair for simple elegance. That really is a most successful dress you are wearing at the moment, for it exactly matches the colour of your eyes. They are the colour of a certain flower – connected, I think, with monks. Fascinating, for you yourself have all the qualities that it would not be advisable for a monk to be in contact with – or am I being irreverent?'

'Yes!' She spoke the word on a startled gasp, for she was suddenly brought up short against a marble stand; she almost toppled the *cloissoné* vase that stood upon it and a broken cry came from her lips. From Paul's lips came a quiet, swift profanity.

'Why do you always behave with me as if I am about to dispossess you of your valued virtue?' he crisped. 'I am a devil, I am ineligible, and heavens, what else? I am really but a man!'

Margo shook her head, and her eyes slipped away from his, to the ivory panelling of the *salon* walls, with almost a silvery sheen to them. Moved on to the fluted columns of the marble fireplace which was screened by silk birds painted so meticulously that they seemed delicately to quiver, held forever in silken flight. The centrepiece of the lovely room was the ivory and gold piano, with cupids holding the candelabra.

And there was Paul, whose own colouring was so in contrast to every object she looked at, desperate to avoid looking at him. Satan in a silver room, she thought wildly.

'I think you need a glass of wine,' he said. 'Our own Chateau Rosé to take the edge off that hysteria I seem to arouse in you. Are you afraid I am going too kiss you again, Miss Jones? Are you afraid that you might forget that you are a virtuous spinster governess, with but one desire – to work?'

'I hate your sarcasm!' she retorted, and tiny flames of colour licked across her cheekbones. They were words that could bring instant dismissal, for he was the man who paid her salary, but she did not regret them, and with a characteristic toss of her head she faced him and dared him to send her away. He merely quirked his eyebrow a shade higher, and then swept an arm towards the door.

'*Accompagnez moi, mademoiselle.*'

'Go with you – where?' Her voice rose a fraction.

'Not to the bedroom,' he drawled, 'but to the cellar. I am going to show you wine from the days of Napoleon, for he drank our wine on some of his most glorious campaigns. I also wish you to become acquainted with the aroma and the bouquet of wine.'

She gave him a questioning look, and the wicked little smile he gave her in return deepened the colour across the fine, smooth modelling of her cheekbones, and made the little shadows underneath more noticeable. He stared intently, and his eyelids seemed weighted by his black lashes, then he flung open the door and indicated that she precede him into the hall. As she walked past him, she gathered the blue skirt of her dress against her, almost a self-protective gesture, as if not even the silk must have contact with him.

'You might feel a little cold down there,' he said. 'Wait a moment, *mademoiselle*. I think there is a shawl of my mother's in the cloakroom.'

He strode across the hall, and returned with a pale-coloured, heavily fringed stole, which being a man he would mistake for a shawl. Margo held out her hand for it, but he stepped behind her and silently, with hands that barely touched her, he draped the beautiful stole about her shoulders. She breathed the Guerlain scent, felt the weight of the fringes, and the silent, alert, tiger-supple figure behind her.

'*Merci, m'sieur.*'

'Turn round,' he ordered.

She did so and he looked her over as if she were in the market and up for sale. Her eyes flashed, and then he smiled. 'You should be painted, Miss Jones. Exactly like that, the *norblaize* hair against the **blue**, the silk fringes against your arms. The result would be most effective.'

'But hardly in keeping with my position in your household, *m'sieur.*' She said it smartly. 'I am a paid servant – the *bonne* of your nephew. And also the colour of my hair offends your mother – I believe she feels that I have a fiery nature to match my hair.'

'But you haven't, of course?' he said sardonically.

'I'm not saying I am demure and scared of my own shadow, but Madame Cassalis considers that a child's companion should have a discreet appearance. If it had not been for the fact that I had impeccable references from Mrs. Van Arden I am sure your mother would never have thought of having me here. I have seen her look at me—' Margo caught her breath on a sigh, for she had a warm heart and didn't enjoy being looked at as if as a working girl she had no right to be attractive or to like a touch of elegance. She bought few clothes, but those she bought were good, and she never wore her hair in the flaunting styles that would have showed off its colour.

'Come, let me show you a portrait of Maman, and then judge her again.' He took Margo firmly by the elbow and led her across the hall to where family portraits were arranged against the dark panelling. She had studied them once or twice in an attempt to understand why the male ancestors bore resemblances to Michel, and even to Desi, yet there was not a sign of the boldly hewn features of Paul, in whose dark face the grey eyes were so striking, so piercing, like the stab of steel. All the Cassalis men, apart from the present master, had aquiline features and dark eyes, with a hint of charm and indulgence about the lips. They had been lean, elegant, and not half as broad in the shoulder as Paul.

Feeling the grip of his fingers, breathing the smoke of his cigar still on his jacket, she had an intense awareness of him. His personality had a frightening touch about it ... she had never felt, when alone with Michel, that he could be ruthless. Not physically ruthless. But Paul was so different. No woman, if he really wanted her, would ever laugh and slip out of his arms.

He brought her to a halt in front of the portraits. 'Look at them,' he said. 'Do you see my mother – not as she is now, but as a girl of your age.'

Margo studied the painted faces of the Cassalis wives and mothers, some of them pretty, some of them elegant, and one or two eager and lovely. She stared and felt a curious jolt of the nerves ... was it possible that the young woman in moss-green velvet, the gown low-necked to display the whiteness of her shoulders and the deep glow of the bronze ringlets against the white skin ... was it really possible that once upon a time Constance Cassalis had been so vital, so alive, and fascinating?

Margo turned her head to look at Paul, and the light above the portraits revealed his own face, with its power and its secret passion. Brooding in that moment, the grey eye hooded by his eyelids, the shadows of his eyelashes across his cheekbones.

'She was lovely, eh?' He spoke dispassionately, his true feelings banked down under the cool and careful voice.

'All the Cassalis brides are painted, and she wore the velvet gown because the skirt was full and concealed the fact that she was pregnant. If you look closely, *mademoiselle*, you will see the defiant fire in her eyes, and see how she holds her head, as if she had just tossed it — defying the world, and the man she had married.'

'Why?' Margo had to ask, she had to know why a lovely bride should look with defiance at the world, as if daring it to accuse her.

'The child she carried was myself, Miss Jones.' And now he looked at Margo, capturing and holding her gaze. 'The man she married was not my father.'

Margo caught her breath . . . he shouldn't be saying these things about his mother . . . and yet he had to, if he was to reveal the true woman who dwelt within that cold proud shell, the hair silvered now, the fire long dead, but not the guilt.

'It was an arranged marriage,' he went on, 'but she was really in love with the son of her father's gamekeeper. Dark as Lucifer, bold as brass, and not to be denied the slim and lovely creature with the dark fire in her hair, and in her heart, who was destined to marry the rich and landed Lucien Cassalis. They had their affair, and though he wanted her to run away with him, she feared to oppose the wishes of her parents. She had been reared to the idea that her husband would be chosen for her, and she saw no recourse, despite her dark lover, but to go through with her marriage to Lucien. To her credit, at least, she was unaware of being with child until a while after her marriage. For years she thought she had fooled Lucien completely, but when he died of a sudden illness, and when his will was read it stated quite firmly that all the land and the properties thereon pertaining to the name of Cassalis were to go to the *rightful* heir of Cassalis land — my brother Michel, and after him to his son should he have one. I work the terraces, Miss Jones. I bring forth the champagne and the wine. I ensure that the chateau remains a perfect example of French architecture. I pay the wages of the wine workers. I give the orders and flourish the phantom whip, but I am only the caretaker of Satancourt and its cellars. If I should marry and have a son, he will never inherit a square inch of Cassalis property. Lucien Cassalis made sure of it.'

Paul Cassalis stood very still and gazed at the portrait of his mother, but there was no harshness stamped on his profile, no resentment that she should have loved unwisely in her lovely youth. But Margo heard him stifle a sigh.

'Lucien had his revenge, and a subtle one, and ever since then Maman has put duty before love. Can you blame her?'

Margo was unsure . . . her own youth, her own warmth of heart, made it difficult for her to understand how all the glory had died out of the heart and soul of Constance Cassalis. She was but a grey shadow of the girl she had been, and it was sad, and a sort of coldness ran over Margo's skin and made her shiver.

'You are cold, despite the shawl?' There was a quizzical note in the voice of the man beside her.

'No.' She stroked the fringes. 'I suppose I am trying to understand the French temperament, the opposition between ardency and logic which must make life rather – difficult.'

'In answer to that, *mademoiselle*, I can only quote Malraux. "A Frenchman is a man who will risk his all on an impulse. But let him stop to consider, and he will not risk a thing." '

'And does that describe you, *m'sieur*?'

'Would you say so, *mademoiselle*?'

'I don't think I have known you long enough to come remotely close to understanding you. One may be able to generalize about a lot of men, but I don't think you come under a general heading. I think you have enormous pride, and you obviously love this place. It must – hurt to know that it can never be truly yours. It must make you feel—' She broke off, for to imply bitterness was to imply that he might harbour resentment towards Desi, and she had seen no sign of this, and the boy had a sort of hero worship of '*mon oncle*', the big man in charge of things.

'Were you about to say that I might be bitter because I have been disinherited?' he drawled, and his voice was closer to her, making her all at once aware that he had drawn her by the arm until she was close enough to see the mercurial glitter of his eyes, and to feel it as if in his fingers, running live and dangerous. 'I am very bitter, that a man should treat me like a son of his own until I am told, on the day of his burial, that I am no such thing. I would sooner have been thrown out of his house than be the recipient of a love that was basically false. I would have left that day, but Michel was still, then, at school, and Maman needed me. I would still have gone if Michel had cared what became of the vine terraces and the chateau—'

'Didn't he care?' She was deeply shocked, somehow, wanting even yet to believe there had been depth to Michel and not merely a hunger for the pleasures of life.

'He cared that there should be money—'

'No!' Her protest wouldn't be silenced. 'How can you say that about him?'

Paul stared down at her, his eyes narrowed, with that peculiar fire flickering inside them. 'How can you know, *mademoiselle*, what a stranger was like? Or was he not a stranger?'

Her heart thumped, her arm twisted in his fingers. 'Let me go!'

'First you will answer my question. Were you one of Michel's girls? He had them scattered up and down

106

France, before and after his marriage. When and where did he meet you – at Cannes?'

His logic was too deadly, his gaze was too threatening, so that the sudden whitening of her face gave her away to him.

'So, at Cannes! Somehow, from the very start, you seemed too good to be true, Miss Jones. An elegant, spirited English girl wishful of being governess to a child in a house so many miles from shops or theatres. I felt there had to be a reason, and so this is it! You were in love with my – with Michel?'

She froze in his grip, and yet she was fired to throw in his face how much the charm of his brother had meant to her. Denial of their association was impossible. She could tell from Paul's face that he would not accept denial. It would infuriate him.

She tossed her hair and a bright lock of it danced free on her forehead. *'Cet animal est très mechant; quand on l'attaque il se défend.'*

'Quite so, *mademoiselle*. Attack me and I strike back. Love Michel and he returned it, eh? In full measure, with all the caressive charm of Don Juan himself.'

'It would be natural for you to hate him,' she flung in his face. 'He was heir to what you wanted. He had it all – the looks, the charm, and the chateau.'

'Don't stop there, *mademoiselle*. Do go on. Say exactly what is in your mind. Say I killed him!'

It was like cold water flung in her face. The flame of quick temper died down, for never for a moment, never for a fleeting shadow of a second had she thought of such a thing – but of course, she hadn't known that Paul Cassalis was not really the owner of Satancourt, only the caretaker until Desi came of age.

She stared at him as silence hung round them, almost palpable, like a curtain enclosing them from the rest of the house and its occupants. Then something stirred within her, almost an ache – pity, compassion, a glimpse of loneliness – but then had not Lucifer been lonely!

'*Pardieu.*' He let her go and looked insolent as he stepped away from her. 'These hands should not touch a woman, eh? It is not honest toil that makes them unspeakable, but their greed for the things that belonged to Michel. A while ago you said that you knew very little about me. Now you know a lot more. In fact we are both in possession of revelations about each other. A most intriguing situation. Will you dare to stay and face it?'

'Will you let me stay?' she retaliated.

'If you went away now, Miss Jones, think of all the joy that would go out of my life.'

'The joy of – of baiting me, *m'sieur*? Of taunting me for coming here to be near Michel's son?'

'Of course,' he drawled. 'What else would I mean?'

What else, indeed! Standing alone now, his hands withdrawn from her, she stood slim and straight and tense, her eyes fixed upon the portrayed face of the man beside his mother. Lean-faced, a little stern, and with the dark eyes of Michel and Desi. Lucien, who had never betrayed while he lived his knowledge of Paul's invidious position in his house. Oh God, but what a way to revenge himself on his wife, by snatching from her son all that the years had taught him to love, to revere – to want. No wonder it no longer mattered to him whether he took a wife or not! Better not to, if he had a son, and that son could never be heir to Satancourt.

The chimes of the hall clock stirred and began to strike the hour of ten.

'You will want to go to bed,' he said, and his voice struck through the chimes and made her start and turn her face to his. Her eyes looked huge, a sort of midnight blue, clouded by her disturbing thoughts and her revolving images.

'No!' Bed was the last place she wanted; she felt too

restless, too shaken, too afraid to lie in the darkness with her thoughts and her images. 'You offered to show me the wine in your cellar.'

'But that was before you learned who and what I am, Miss Jones.'

'Don't mock me! I am not a child, *m'sieur*, to be shocked by what women do for love.'

'No, perhaps you wouldn't be – having loved my brother. Come, then. We go this way.' He led her across the hall, so quiet again now the lock had ceased to break the silence with its chimes. Shadows fell around them, then came the click of a door being opened and the softer click of a light switched on, bright against the steep and slightly damp cellar steps. The smell that arose and struck at Margo was curiously repellent for a moment, and then curiously inviting, a mixture of the alcohol, the sugars, the acids and salts that were elemental in the wine. It was, she thought, like entering an alchemist's lair, a drape of cobwebs where the stone pillars supported the arch of the roof.

The *chai* of Satancourt, with rack upon rack of bottled wine, the long necks poking forward out of the dimness, with a gleam of silver, red, and blue bottle caps.

There was a gleam of chain, which had probably been used to clean the inside of the polished oak barrels. There was a shelf where the pipettes lay like glass things from out of a surgery. 'Learning about wine is like learning about women,' Paul was saying. 'It takes time and instinct—'

There he broke off as Margo's heel suddenly slid on the steps and she cried out as she lost her balance. She felt herself falling and fear was a lurch of the heart, and then a grip of arms so strong and painful that she gasped again.

'You could break your neck!'

Her head flung back on her slender neck and her eyes

were shocked. He stared down at her, then he bent his head and his mouth was on her mouth, and the overhead light flung their embraced shadow high up the stone wall. She let herself be kissed, and she felt the anger – the anger against himself and against her, as he raked his fingers into her copper hair and bent her head sideways so that he could end his kiss in the soft hollow under her earlobe.

'You are too damned beautiful for a governess,' he snarled. 'From the start I knew that and I should have kicked you out that first day. Now he cares, eh? The boy cares? He has to have you, or break that small heart of his. Damn you, Margo Jones! Why couldn't you stay away from us?'

'I – I'd like nothing better than to be able to stay away from you,' she gasped. 'Why can't you leave me alone? I didn't come here – down here to be – you're hateful, Paul! You take advantage!'

'Better to break your neck, eh? Or you think so. Well, a kiss is soon forgotten, and it was grab you or let you be hurt. Not even the devil's kiss could hurt more than a cracked or broken bone.' He stared with narrow, flickering eyes at her disarrayed hair, flaming dark about the whiteness of her face – white but for the blue fury of her eyes. 'Yes, he'd want you, with his eye for beauty. But did it not hurt when he walked out on you?'

She flinched and wanted to strike at the dark face that only moments ago had been so close to hers, warm and hard, the strong chin thrusting at her throat as he kissed under her earlobe. Damn him!

'I'm not Michel's cast-off!' she cried, the words echoing through the *chai*. 'If you take me for that sort—'

'*Non.*' He shook his head, thrusting the black hair from his brow with an impatient movement of his hand. The light caught the gold band of his signet ring and now she saw clearly that the device was not the same as the one over the entrance to the chateau. It was a black rose against the gold – *norblaize* – and probably connected with his mother's family.

Because fate had bedevilled him, did he have to play the devil with every woman who came within his grasp? She turned wild eyes to the steps and wanted to leave this wine cloister, with the great shadow of Paul looming up the wall with its coating of white over the stone.

'You will taste the wine before you go,' then he laughed in his throat. 'Or should I say before you flee like the proverbial chaste maiden? It is the first wine that I was directly responsible for and put down a year before my – before Lucien died. It has a certain youthfulness and zest, but then, you see, I was not always the satyr I see reflected in your eyes, *mademoiselle*. In those days we tramped the wine in the great vats, we danced and splashed in the juice as it ran from the skins, until we were like savages who had been to a killing.' He laughed again and walked to the racks that rose to the ceiling. He reached up and grasped the neck of a bottle, and she watched helplessly, almost like a moth that wanted the sear of the flame.

'Young days, good days,' he went on, holding up the long-necked bottle, capped in red, so that the wine inside caught the light. 'We toiled in the yard from dawn to dusk, and energy burst from our pores as the yeast burst from the grapes. Hot days, *mademoiselle*, with a haze dancing with insects and the cicadas shrill in the trees. How fat the grapes, and bunched, like the ringlets of a girl ready for love. How good to rest a while in the shade of a tree, with bread, onion and cheese, and a long swig of wine. How good the smells, of oxen and the raw bouquet from the vats, and the sudden tang of cologne from the long black hair of one of the grape-pickers.'

He swung to face Margo and there were laughing, mocking, careless devils in his grey eyes. 'The grape-pickers were girls, and I was young and warm and perhaps a little wild, and I liked girls. So what?' He shrugged his wide shoulders and his lean fingers tore the foil from the bottle and jerked out the wine-darkened cork without the aid of a corkscrew.

So strong, she thought, backing against the white wall so that the skirt of her blue dress flared against the white like a bright fan. The silk fringes of the stole danced against the bare skin of her arms, and she felt him looking at her through his lashes as he took a pair of wine tasters from a shelf and holding them by the stems filled them from the bottle.

'*Voilà!*' The wine was a dark rose colour, glinting like rubies gone to liquid through the fine thin glass of the slender tasting glasses. He set aside the bottle and came to her with the filled glasses. 'Here you are, *mademoiselle*. The distilled youth of Paul Cassalis. Will you dare to drink of him?'

'You are always daring me to do something, *m'sieur.*' As she reached for the proffered glass she prayed that her hand wouldn't tremble and reveal her state of nerves. '*Merci.*'

'You are welcome, *mademoiselle*, to whatever I have.'

She flicked a look at him, and saw the sardonic humour etched around his lips. Here amidst the wine, and the bare blaze of light, his broad back to a column, he had the look of a freebooter. 'The woman is the goblet, the man is the wine,' he said, and he nosed the wine he had put down in the days – the young far-off days – when he had believed himself the heir to the chateau and the *chai*. She touched her lips to the rim of the glass and she breathed the wine and she caught her breath. Roses, she thought. The deep crushy scent of high-summer roses, dark-petalled, slumbrous in the sun. She sipped the wine – and it was sweet! Darkly, intoxicatingly sweet!

'Well?' he murmured, as if he knew full well her secret reaction to *his* wine. 'And what do you think of the *vigne rosé*?'

'Excellent, *m'sieur*.'

'To the devil with polite phrases,' he snarled at her again. 'Tell the truth for once!'

'I always tell the truth.'

'Little liar. You came to Satancourt under the robe, and you know it. You wanted something of Michel in Desi. Now you have something of me in that glass you hold, so tell me what you think, and don't spare my feelings or my blushes.'

'If you ever blushed,' and suddenly she laughed and it must have been the effect of the wine, 'it must have been when you were a baby and your nurse forgot to test your bath water before putting you in it.'

'Very likely – if you can picture me as a baby.'

She couldn't, and she gave him a quick look as he stood there in his dark dress trousers and dark jacket opened against a shirt of thick white silk. That uncontrollable jag of hair was black against his forehead again, and his glance as it locked with hers was steel-grey. Only to his mother had he ever been a baby, and each time Constance held him, or looked at him, she must have remembered her wild young lover, and faced the awful fear that Lucien knew that Paul was not his son. Then as the years went by and Lucien had not spoken—

'How did Lucien Cassalis learn of it – that you were not—?' The words left her lips before she could hold them back. 'I know I shouldn't ask such a thing, but how could he be so certain if your mother never breathed a word.'

'There was a robbery at the chateau, about a year before Lucien died. A box of jewellery was stolen from Maman's room. It was one of those antique boxes with a secret drawer, and finding it bulky the thief threw it into the trees. It appeared to be empty when a servant found it, but Lucien found the secret compartment and there were letters in it – the indiscreet kind that women keep, and sometimes forget that they have kept in their own handwriting revelations best destroyed. They were love notes returned by her lover. She had asked for them when she married Lucien and he had given them back. She should have destroyed them, but as fate would have it, she did not. Lucien never revealed that he had read them until after his death, in a letter to Maman left with his will and testament. He saw no way, he said, to leave Cassalis property to her lover's child. To do so would rob Michel, whom he knew to be his own son. Frenchmen are forever logical, Miss Jones. And who could argue with such logic, despite the fact that Lucien knew how little Michel cared about Satancourt.'

She swallowed the strange, bitter sadness of his words with the dark sweetness of the wine, then he took the empty glass and they left the *chai.*

When they reached the stairs he paused there and drew the stole from her shoulders. His fingers crushed the silk and he half-lifted it to his nostrils as if to breathe the scent on it.

'Don't judge me too harshly, Miss Jones.' It was not a plea, nor yet an order. 'I am just one of those men whom fate selects to make half a devil of. I think you might understand better than most why I can't always be gentle or tolerant. The fabric of your character is not flimsy, *mademoiselle.* You look deep, you seek answers, and you care that others should be – happy. Is this not true?'

She stood there looking up at him, and then she mounted a couple of stairs so that she might be level with his eyes, but he turned them aside and gazed at a tapestry on the wall, and it was his profile at which she looked. Forceful, with a deep line carved at the side of his mouth ... the mouth which only a short while ago had forced submission from hers.

He wasn't gentle, yet she had seen him show kindness to Desi, and indulgence towards Céleste. And those grape-picking girls with the long scented hair had loved the wild, dark youth he had been. 'I am never sure of how you are judging me,' she half-smiled. 'A short while ago you said that you wished you had kicked me out before Desi grew to depend on me. Don't you like to be depended upon, *m'sieur*? You know very well that you are the mainspring of Satancourt, and surely what matters is that we give of our best regardless of whether we do it for ourselves or for others. Can't you forgive Lucien Cassalis, for having too much pride? After all, you once loved him—'

'Love, Miss Jones?' Paul drew away from the stairs, and his mouth was twisted in a sardonic smile. 'I don't know that I trust love any more – do you? We can both say, can't we, that we have been kicked in the teeth by it.'

Then, before Margo could answer him, he inclined his head in a mocking little bow, then turned on his heel and walked off into the shadows. She heard his footfalls echoing along the covered walk that led out into the courtyard. They had a strange loneliness about them, dying away from her until everything was quiet again, and she stood alone but for the armoured knight across the hall that gazed blankly at her silent figure in the blue dress which Paul had said was the colour of her eyes.

When she reached the gallery she paused to gaze down into the shadowy hall, and through an open window nearby she breathed the night scents that drifted in from the grounds of the chateau. Her face was pensive as she stood there by the balustrade, for tonight she had a new feeling about Satancourt.

It wasn't just another house. another residence in which she would work for as long as it pleased the Cassalis family. It had an atmosphere of its very own; an appeal to the the senses as well as the imagination. It lived on while those who had created it, adding year by year to its grace, had long since become only faces with painted eyes in old-gold frames.

Nothing stirred, and yet she almost heard in the silence the echo of a girlish laugh, and the sound of an old song.

Margo went on her way to Desi's room and took a quiet look at him. He was sleeping fast in this great house that would one day be his to cherish ... or would he be indifferent to its history and its grace?

As Margo proceeded to her rooms on the upper floor, the lines of a certain verse were running through her mind:

'The place still speaks of worn-out beauty of roses.
  And half retrieves a failure of Bergamotte.

Rich light and a silence so rich one all but supposes
  The voice of the clavichord stirs to a dead gavotte.'

CHAPTER SEVEN

THERE came an afternoon when Margo discovered an interesting lichened stairway leading down to a gazebo that stood alone near the lake. As she stood above on the steps looking down at it, and as she caught the sound of the water rustling among the reeds, it seemed to her the perfect place for lovers to meet. It had a steep, curly-tiled roof which gave it a Chinese look, and the windows were arched, and she could just glimpse the potted palm trees inside, their leaves all tangled together to make it the perfect rendezvous.

Desi took his nap in the coolness of his room, and she was alone and carrying a volume of Shelley, the perfect poet for a lazy, sunlit afternoon.

She took a step forward on to the stairway, and then she stiffened, for surely she had glimpsed a movement in the gazebo, a gleam of white. She hesitated. If a member of the family was there, then it would be an intrusion, and she had grown wary of intruding, of finding herself alone again with Paul Cassalis.

Then as she stood hesitant the person clad in white came out from the little pavilion. It was a man, and in his crisp linen suit he stood gazing at the lake and a breath of wind caught at his smooth dark hair and he lifted his face as if to feel that breeze on his skin ... and Margo caught her breath and in her surprise the book of poems fell from her hand and went tumbling down the steps.

He turned smartly, that man by the lakeside, and then he stooped as the book fell at his feet. He picked it up, glanced at the title on the spine, and then allowed his eyes to lift and rest on Margo, caught in an attitude of surprise there at the top of the steps. His eyes flicked her uniform, and then her uncapped hair, sheened by the sun. He smiled slowly, and he was every bit as good-looking as she remembered him.

'*Bonjour, mademoiselle. Comment vous portez-vous?*'

'*Bien, merci, et vous-même?*'

'Most deliciously surprised.' He quirked an eyebrow. 'Shall I come up there, or will you come down to me?'

'I don't know your name, *m'sieur*.'

'Reserved as ever, eh?' His smile was slow and attractive. 'My name is Raoul d'Arcy. I had no idea that day at Nantes airport that you were coming here – so you, I see, are the *bonne* of the boy?'

'And you are his Uncle Raoul.' After the first jolt of surprise, Margo found herself walking down the steps to join him. So the worldly Parisian who made those clever soldiers for Desi, the man who enjoyed talking of his *amours* with Paul, was the same man who had wanted to give her a lift in his car that day she had arrived in France to take up her post at Satancourt. It was a small world, and she couldn't help but smile as she extended a hand for her book. Instead he took her hand and bending his head he kissed her fingers.

'You shouldn't do that, *m'sieur*.' She snatched back her hand and put it behind her. 'Someone might see you. Madame Cassalis is rather strict about these things.'

'Who has given her cause to be strict – Paul?' With seeming casualness Raoul opened the book, which she had taken from the library in preference to a novel. There seemed enough drama at Satancourt, and she had hoped for a peaceful hour with Shelley, whose poetry could play on the senses like silk on the skin. Soothing, with an underplay of sensuousness. Poor brilliant Shelley, who had been so handsome, so tormented by love.

'So you were coming to the gazebo to read love poems.' Raoul shot a quick look at her face, but he wasn't mocking her. 'How do you like being employed as *bonne* to the heir of all this, including a brand of champagne which is now being served at all the best tables? Paul has a flair — *non?*'

'I have tasted some of his wine, *m'sieur.*' She remembered, and she turned aside her face to the cool breeze blowing across the lake. 'I am not a connoisseur, of course, but the wine was memorable.'

'Yes, wine should have that quality — as a woman should have it. May I say that I kept on thinking of you, with your unusual hair, and eyes of a blue I have not seen very often. A Frenchman always makes the mistake of thinking that all English girls are fair—'

'I am partly Welsh,' she said quickly, for it was a matter of pride with her. 'My name is Jones — Margo Jones.'

'Margo,' he murmured. 'Shortened from Marigold, eh? Because of the hair?'

'My parents were never that whimsical, *m'sieur,* or that hopeful. I am just Margo.'

'You say it so modestly.' His eyes were amused. 'It is something I have noticed about British women — the nicest of them. They have such a delicious unawareness of how seductive they are. My elegant countrywomen are all too aware of their charms.'

'Are you a great authority on the charms of women, *m'sieur?*' She was amused in her turn, remembering the sardonic note in Paul's voice when he had said that his friend Raoul was a great talker.

'No Frenchman, *mademoiselle,* is born without a dash of original sin,' he said, and again she thought of Paul — the devil in a silver room. Raoul gestured at the gazebo. 'Pretty, eh? There are always these exciting little hideaways in and around the precincts of a true French chateau. Do you like the place?'

She nodded and glanced from the lake to the slenderly

sculptured turrets of Satancourt, coned by their dark, sunlit tiles. The pennant of the house had a proud quiver to it, high up there against the burning blue of the sky. 'It is a lovely, dreamlike place,' she said.

'But there are shadows,' he murmured. 'Being half Welsh and a little of a witch you would be aware of the – ghosts.'

Her gaze dwelt on the veranda which she knew to be Maxine's. She had wondered at first why they, the family, allowed the young widow to go on living in a suite that overlooked the lake. Then she had realized that to deprive her of seeing the lake whenever she felt the need would intensify her sense of loss. Ghosts! Yes, for Maxine a lean and handsome shadow still dwelt in the silver water, and perhaps she saw him at times, coming to her with his hair damp and that gleam of desire in his eyes.

'I have not yet met the mother of my – of Desi,' she said. 'I am told that she is not yet recovered from the tragedy.'

'Nor ever will be, in the fullest sense,' he sighed. 'Paul, for all his force, will not force her to face reality. Paul has his own strange understanding of what it feels like to suffer a body blow. Well, Margo Jones, what do you think of Paul Etienne Cassalis?'

She didn't know how to answer the man who was his friend. She could only say: 'There are many facets to him, and I feel that one would have to know him a long time before making up one's mind whether he is to be – trusted.'

'A provocative remark, *mademoiselle*.' Raoul's eyes narrowed as if suddenly he saw behind her femininity and realized that she had a mind and was more than capable of using it. 'So you have judged him?'

'Not exactly, but when something much valued is taken from a very proud and possessive man it can sometimes set loose – devils.'

'And the witch in you, Margo, has glimpsed the devils – or have you sampled one of them?' Curiosity flickered in Raoul's eyes. 'Paul is not unattractive to women, though he has little of the polish that made Michel such a *succès fou* with the women.'

She flinched, for she was learning the hard way that Michel had not loved her for *herself*, but had been a natural born lover of pretty women. 'I think both he and his brother inherited their fire from Madame. When I first met her – it is so hard now to glimpse the beauty that she was. The bonework is there, of course, but the fire has gone to ash. Paul bears a black rose on his signet ring, and he grows those *norblaize* roses in his private garden – there is dark passion in his blood, is there not, M'sieur d'Arcy?'

Raoul flung out his hands in a very Gallic gesture. 'She came of a family much older, even, than Lucien Cassalis'. It had wild seeds, violent roots, great beauty in its women, and as you say – dark passion. Over the years Madame has tried to forget her own youth, her own wild fling of freedom before she was bound by the chains of the marriage arranged for her. Duty and desire waged their own war within her, and duty won the battle. What a great pity – ah, I see from the flash to your eyes that you are with me, Margo!'

'Yes.' The thought had leapt from his mind to hers. 'What a pity Michel was not her firstborn.'

'*Le destin* plays strange tricks, eh? Michel should have loved his inheritance, but instead he loved only women. It is Paul – Paul the outcast – who loves the inheritance.'

'I wonder,' she murmured, her gaze upon the still silver waters of the lake, which had long since washed itself free of Michel's blood, 'what he will do when the boy comes of age. Will he go away, do you think?'

Raoul didn't answer for what seemed the longest time, and he studied the silhouette of Satancourt against the brightness of the sky, etched there by a master hand, to stand or fall according to its master.

'If I were Paul,' he said at last, 'I could not endure for a second time to see all this pass into other hands, but devils have been martyrs as well as saints, Margo Jones. There is no knowing at this date what sort of a man Desi will grow into. If he takes after his father, then Paul will stay. He will give his life to the place – or so I believe.'

'Stone and tile, tree and vine,' she murmured. 'And these are what he loves?'

Raoul glanced at the volume of Shelley poetry. 'You believe in a warmer love, being a woman. Very much a woman, I might add. Has Paul noticed?'

'His admiration is for stone and vine,' she fenced.

'But when passion calls he can't embrace them. Paul might love his cloister but he isn't a monk – is he, Margo?'

'You are getting personal, *m'sieur*. The child's *bonne* has to mind her place, and that is in the nursery suite. If you will give me the book—'

'I will not, *mademoiselle la bonne*. I am going to request that you join me for iced lime in the coolness of Paul's garden. He lets me have the pleasure of it – and you also, if you have seen the *norblaize* roses? *Oui?*'

'I have filched a look, that is all, *m'sieur*. He has never invited me into his garden—'

'Rose garden of the Devil, you are thinking?' Raoul looked at her with knowing Gallic eyes. 'I must see you there, clad in that virtuous uniform, all prim and starched on the outside, and deep – deep like the rose on the inside.'

'Are you an artist?' Suddenly she had guessed, and laughed at herself for thinking he might be anything else. The soldiers – the way he expressed himself – the obvious liking for the company of a woman! 'But you don't paint. I think you make rather lovely and fascinating things with your hands. Am I right, *m'sieur?*'

'Yes, witch.' He gave a chuckle; an attractive, masculine sound. 'That is how Paul and I met. I went to a *chai* on the Breton coast to find models for my work. Wine workers, dashing and handsome creatures. Oxen and bare brown limbs. He was twenty and so was I. For fifteen years we have been friends. *I* trust him.'

'*Touchée.*' She said it lightly, but her face was touched by melancholy for a fleeting moment. Twenty, and with the warm blood of ambition racing like wine through his veins ... turning cold, cold as ice-water when he learned a year later that he was not to be the master of Satancourt, only its slave.

She thought of him in the cool stone *chai*, with the racks of bottles and the casks of wine piled up like a smugglers' hoard. Paul was too strong, too proud to be a slave, and standing there in the sunlight she felt her own blood run cold. Had he not asked her outright if she thought he had killed Michel? Had the suspicion not crept, and crept closer each time she came to the lake ... as if something were trying to reach out to warn her there was danger in the very air she breathed in the company of Paul Cassalis?

'Are you staying at Satancourt?' she asked Raoul d'Arcy. 'Or have you only come for the day?'

'I have an apartment here and I come and go.' He stared openly at Margo. 'I think I shall stay awhile, perhaps to do some work on some wall cameos which are to adorn the bedroom of a certain rich bride. You give me ideas, Margo. You have a Botticelli face, with a touch of earth and heaven in it. Would you mind if I allowed you to inspire me?'

'Would you take a scrap of notice if I said I did mind?' She smiled a little, and felt a quick stab of gladness that he was staying. He was the kind of man who enjoyed saying daring things to a woman ... unlike Paul he would

would never carry them out.

'An artist has licence to make a woman immortal if he wishes. Look at the Mona Lisa.'

'I once heard a rumour that the model was a man,' she said, a dent of humour showing beside her lips. 'Is there any truth in it?'

'Have you been to the Louvre?' Raoul leaned his shoulders against a willow tree and the long leaves brushed darkly green against his white linen.

'Yes, I did go – oh, about five years ago, at a time when I was feeling rather blue. Did I go in the wrong mood?'

'Not at all. Such works of art should be seen with eyes opened wide to the distress as well as the bliss of love.' Raoul plucked a leaf and stroked his mouth with it. 'Was the man already married?'

'No – yes. By the time I went to Paris he was married.'

'He was a Frenchman?'

'Yes.'

'The alliance already arranged when you met him?'

'I was young – and romantic.'

'And does the torch still burn?'

'No—' The word came so voluntarily that she was deeply shaken by her own sense of surprise. 'No, it must have gone out and I didn't notice. The resilience of youth, I suppose. I imagine what lingered was the sense of loneliness—'

'You were lonely? *Pauvre petite*, if only I had been around to console you!'

'*Rien à faire*,' she smiled. 'In a way I was quite content. I had my work. There is, after all, more to life than love.'

'*Nom d'un chien!*' Raoul looked quite horrified by her statement. 'When love ceases to be the sweet heart of life, then you may call me a husk of a man. What are you saying, that you are going to give that body, those eyes, that dark flame of hair, into the arms of a career? *Non, jamais!* I shall marry you myself—'

'Don't be a fool!' She turned swiftly and her hair swished over her left eye as she ran up the steps to the grounds of the chateau. She heard him running after her and she laughed to herself, for she was quite sure that it wasn't often that a woman ran away from him. She had to elude him and she ran without thinking towards a grilled iron door. She pulled it open and ran inside, and then as the roses blazed at her and their scent sprang a trap for the senses Margo realized that she had entered the sanctum of the *norblaize* roses. She turned to run out again, but Raoul was there in the entrance, and his eyes were alight with the chase, and with the wicked delight of having her 'gone to earth' in this walled garden.

'Well, pretty fox, what do you do now?' he teased, closing the iron-laced door behind him and standing there with his back to it. For an instant, lean and white-clad, he reminded her of Michel, and she was stunned that she had ever thought of Michel as a very rare member of the human race. How young she had been ... how unaware of what rarity really was!

'I am waiting for my glass of iced lime,' she said. 'It cools the blood, does it not?'

He laughed and pressed his shoulders against the iron, like a dark cat arching its back at a stroking hand. 'Is that all you want, *petite renarde*?'

'Mmmm.' Margo knelt on a patch of soft, clovered grass and cupped a dark red rose in her hands. It was exquisite, the petals curled around the hidden heart with all the precision of chiselled jewels, with all the softness of damask. 'I can hardly believe that *he* grows these lovely things, yet he does.'

'Beauty and the devil.'

She twisted her body to look at Raoul, unafraid to see him there against the sun, a lithe and attractive man, but without the smouldering black-rose passion distilled into the blood from the bold and violent past. 'So you do know, *m'sieur*, that he can be a devil?'

Raoul shrugged his shoulders and came towards her. 'Is anyone an angel, *mademoiselle*? Are you afraid that Paul might ever hurt that boy?'

'It's unthinkable!'

'You have grown fond of Desi, eh? He is very like Michel to look at.'

'So – so I am told.' She released the rose and was careful of the thorns as she drew her hands away. 'How beautiful and cruel is the rose, *m'sieur*. Like an enchanted princess guarded by spikes of iron.'

'You have much imagination, Margo.'

She stood up and brushed a wrinkle from the skirt of her uniform. 'And I am not to let my imagination run away with me, is that what you mean?'

'Yes. Satancourt is a very old place, with its roots in the past and its spires in the sky, and it excites strange thoughts. More than once it has witnessed tragedy, and these shadows linger in the sunlight, and they deepen when twilight falls. It is then that the imagination starts to play tricks, when the stars gleam like eyes in the lake, and the rustle of a tree takes on the sound of a restless spirit.'

'Don't – please!' She gave a little shiver, and looked about her at the velvety roses aglow in their webbing of thorns. They seemed strange companions for a ruthless man, and yet when she recalled the biting temper of his kisses their thorns seemed all too symbolic. He could stroke and scratch at the same time, and he did it without really caring.

Margo shot a look at her watch. 'I really must go to Desi,' she said, 'perhaps you will let me join you for a drink some other time – if you have really decided to stay?'

'It would take wild horses to drag me away.' He stood aside from the iron door and he smiled into her eyes. 'I truly hoped that we would meet again. Dare I hope that you are glad?'

'I think I am,' she said honestly. 'You and I are of the world beyond the gate of Satancourt; we have no personal part in the drama, and that makes a sort of bond between us.'

'*Vive le* bond!' He took her hand and looked at its slenderness, and its pallor against his own. 'Whenever I hold the hand of a woman I am amazed by those who imagine there is not a great deal of difference between women and men. There is half a world of difference, *dieu soit loué!*'

She laughed a little and took from him the book of poems. 'I had planned such a peaceful siesta alone with Shelley.'

'Peace is for the elderly, and you and I are not yet out of our emotional breeches.'

'*M'sieur!*'

'A shocked look becomes you, *mademoiselle.*'

'*Au'voir,*' she said severely, and went on her way towards the courtyard. She had reached the bank of deep pink oleanders, scenting the air with their bitter-almond smell, when someone came round from the other side and almost knocked her down. 'Oh!' A hand reached out swiftly and as she recovered her balance she felt the warm hard fingers gripping her arm, and the grey eyes stabbing down at her. The oleanders spiked the air with their dangerous perfume, great pretty flowers with poison in their stems.

'I almost knocked you over!'

'You stride so swiftly – silently – like a tiger!'

The air about them panted with heat, with perfume, with breathless expectancy. His eyes glittered as they swept her startled face, and the loosened spun-copper hair. His mouth took on not hardness but a sudden mocking indulgence, and he bent his tall head to breathe her skin and hair.

'You smell of roses,' he drawled against her temple. 'Have you been trespassing in my garden?'

'I'm afraid so.' Her heart was beating so swiftly that she could barely breathe; she could feel his warm skin, and the tang of his clean, hard-worked masculinity was strong in her nostrils. Everything swam around her, as if the heat of the day suddenly struck at her, and there was no fight only a drugged acceptance as he suddenly pulled her among the oleanders. He took her hair in his fist and used the thick silky strand like a rope to pull her to him. His other hand caressed her shoulder and she felt tiny shock-waves of desire running over her skin, playing over it as his fingers played, ripples of acute sensitivity that made her want more – much more.

She had to struggle free of his hold, break free of his touch, end the traitorous pleasure her body found with him . . . out of its loneliness, its lack of love since the loss of Michel.

It was Michel she loved . . . he had brought her heart alive . . . Paul held only her weak feminine body in his arms.

'*Embrasse-moi*,' he murmered, and his voice was thick, like the lashes clustering about his eyes. 'Kiss me, *femme norblaize*.'

'God – no!' She had to break free of the lethargy, the desire to please him – *yes*, please him, this strong, dark creature whom she distrusted with every particle of her heart. She tried to turn her head aside, but he did not spare her the pain of pulled hair. 'You devil – *devil*!'

'My dear, your indignation is most attractive, but why fight me when you long to give in to me?'

'Y-you'd make me like that other one – that other girl who worked here – who ended up in the lake!' Margo pushed at his shoulders, feeling the hard thrust of the muscles under the thin stuff of his shirt, open to his chest where the saint medal was meshed in the black crucifix of hair. Her senses spun – she hated him even as she wanted him. *Love?* It was surely a desecration of the word and all it stood for to apply it to this wild reaction of the senses. There was no tenderness in his face, seen through her blaze of anger and torment. It was brown and merciless, so that the sudden flash of his teeth was brute-white.

'Don't laugh at me!' She reached for his eyes with fingers tensed to claw the mockery out of the silver-grey irises and the black pupils.

'You are enough to make a saint laugh, let alone a devil.' He caught her hand and forced it down against his throat, where the skin was hot and smooth and laid like silk over the beating veins. 'What the hell are you thinking? That the wretched girl killed herself for love of me? She jumped in the lake out of sheer wanton temper, making sure she did it when I would be riding by on my way to the terraces. I saw she had chosen the shallow part where the reeds are, so I left her there to be pulled out by the boatman. *Comprenez-vous, mademoiselle?*'

She stared up at him, a tearmark on her cheek, and no comprehension at all in her eyes. 'I was told – I thought—'

'I don't happen to be fired to frantic desire by every female I look at, Miss Jones. Occasionally a female looks my way and when I don't look back – well, must I go into complete details? Are you so innocent that you don't know what I am saying?'

'You mean the girl had to find some way to make you notice her?'

'The penny falls! For an intelligent creature you are sometimes very obtuse. Am I so distasteful that you cannot comprehend of someone feeling a fancy for me? Is that it?'

She didn't answer directly, for she was thinking of the way she had been told about that girl and her leap into the lake. Yvonne had wanted her to believe that the girl had died. She had implanted the seed of distrust, quite intentionally, and the thing had rooted, and Margo needed a minute or two to adjust to this sudden violent weeding out.

Abruptly Paul released her, letting go her hair and her body in one swift movement. It was so unexpected, so sudden, that all she could do was go on staring at him, wordlessly. He quirked a black eyebrow, and then he thrust his hands into the pockets of his breeches. 'Your silence is eloquent, Miss Jones. I apologize for imposing my touch on your cool virtuous skin. But you aren't really burned. I leave no scars if I can help it, and I would truly hate to mark that lovely body of yours.

He spun on his heel and walked away, and all that was left was the bittersweet perfume of the oleanders, and the stifled cry on Margo's lips. She backed for support against a tree, for her legs felt suddenly so odd, as if they might give way beneath her. She stared for a long moment into the heart of one of the great pink flowers and it was as if she were looking into her own heart and seeing there an unbearable truth. When her strength returned she made her way into the chateau and before going upstairs to the nursery she paused in front of a wall mirror and smoothed her hair with a hand that still shook slightly.

The truth which had come to her with such pain was there in her eyes, and she turned away quickly, and almost failed to notice Madame Cassalis standing on the stairs.

'There you are, Miss Jones! I thought you would be with Desi – may I inquire where you have been? It is past four o'clock and time for him to have his tea.'

'I went for a stroll, *madame*, while he slept. I didn't

notice the time—'

Madame Cassalis stared at Margo, whose face was rather white so that her eyes seemed immense and darkly blue. Margo gazed back at Paul's mother, whom she could no longer think of as a cold, distant woman whose feelings were petrified. This woman had loved, and in return that love had tortured her and her eldest son.

'Are you quite happy here at Satancourt, Miss Jones?'

It was the first time Madame Cassalis had asked such a question and for a moment Margo felt the treacherous stab of tears at the back of her eyes. If only it were possible to tell this woman that she understood a little of what she had been through ... that she knew of her secret with regard to Paul.

Paul, who had been reared to believe a cruel lie, only to have the cruel truth thrown in his face without a moment's warning. Margo knew that his mother would never forgive herself for that, and had grown so harsh with herself that she could no longer feel, or give way to gentler feelings.

'Go to the child,' she said. 'When he has had his tea, you are to make him tidy for a visit to his *maman*. You will go with him. Maxine has asked to see you.'

'Has she really, *madame*?' Margo was pleasantly surprised. 'I never expected—'

'Nor I, Miss Jones, but it would seem Desi has been prattling about you and Maxine asked only a short while ago to see his *bonne* with the pretty hair.'

Margo flushed, for between Madame Cassalis and herself there lingered the memory of their first interview, and that rather inhuman request that she keep her hair covered. Margo knew the reason now; the colour reminded Madame too vividly of her own red-bronze hair when a girl ... a passionate, wilful, rebellious girl, aware that she must marry a man she didn't love, while her own wild lover roamed the grounds and woods of her home, the son of her father's gamekeeper, black-haired and wilful as herself.

'Go now.' Madame Cassalis reverted to a sharp tone of voice, as if she regretted showing a little humanity towards Margo. 'And do wear your cap when you are on duty, Miss Jones. Loosened hair looks so – so–' She walked away quickly, without completing her reprimand, and Margo raised a hand to her hair. The roots of it still tingled from Paul's grip upon her hair, as if it were a silk rope about her neck, useful for pulling a woman close to his hard brown body.

To escape the memory of that encounter she ran all the way upstairs to Desi, and they were half-way through their nursery tea when the door opened and Raoul d'Arcy entered, carrying a box under his arm. *'Bonjour, bon soldat!* And how is my young friend?'

Desi leapt from his chair and ran to hug Raoul around the waist. 'I didn't know you were here, Uncle Raoul! Grand'mère didn't tell me, nor did Margo.'

He cast a conspiratorial look at Margo, who sat back in her chair and smiled at Desi's delighted reception of this impeccably clad man who looked slightly out of place in a child's nursery. 'I expect your *bonne* forgot all about me,' he drawled. 'She probably had other business which took her mind off me.'

Her smile faltered and her pulse-rate quickened. Had he seen her with Paul? Was he intimating that he had witnessed Paul's abduction of her into the oleander bushes? Her fingers tensed about the handle of her teacup and she strove not to lose her composure, readjusted with her cap and the smooth knot of hair at her nape.

'Won't you join us for cream *vol-au-vent, m'sieur,* topped with a preserved strawberry? Desi loves them.'

'Desi is a little boy, *mademoiselle,* but I am a big one.' His lip quirked and she knew from the slightly wicked gleam in his eyes that he had followed her from the rose garden and he had seen Paul take hold of her. She tilted her chin, for already she had sworn to herself that never, never again would Paul catch her at a disadvantage. From now on she was on the defensive as never before in her life, and this resolve gave to her eyes a burning blueness. Raoul looked into them and for an instant the fun was swept from his lean face.

'All afternoon I have been searching for something to drink,' he said. 'A cup of tea would be very welcome.'

'*Oui, m'sieur*. Will you take a chair?'

He cast a quizzical look at the cane armchairs, and instead lowered his frame to a big square floor-cushion. Desi knelt beside him and accepted eagerly the box which Raoul had brought him. 'What is it?' he demanded.

'Look and see, *mon ami*.' Raoul stretched his legs and glanced about the nursery. 'I detect a few changes, *mademoiselle*. The last time I was here the room had more formality. Has your British hand been at work as well as your heart?'

'Desi and I found some bits and pieces of furniture in the attics which we rather liked. Those cane chairs for example, and the floor-cushions, and the curtains with the spiky flowers on them.' She came to him with a cup of tea. 'I hope you approve?' She handed him the cup and held the sugar-bowl so he could help himself if he so wished.

'*Merci*, but no sugar. I could develop a "pot", being no longer in my twenties and not having those hanging gardens of Bacchus to climb like Paul. Yes, I do approve of the little touches of informality. I believe that a child's life should be a little rumpled – like a woman's hair.'

'Look, *mademoiselle*!' Desi ran to her and showed her the large, perfect replica of a *chasseur d'Afrique* which Raoul had carved, painted and dressed for the boy. 'Is it not *magnifique*? Is not Uncle Raoul a clever man?'

'Very clever, *mon petit*.' She took the soldier into her hands and studied it; the uniform was exact in every detail and very dashing, and then she caught her breath, for the face under the *kepi* bore a startling resemblance to Michel. She glanced at Raoul and he was studying her, a narrowed look to his eyes.

'The face is familiar?' he murmured.

'Yes – he looks like Desi. But tell me, *m'sieur*, why must you always give him soldiers? Why not bus conductors or policemen?'

'A good question, *mademoiselle*.' Raoul smiled and looked at Desi. 'Well, *mon ami*, would you like it if I gave you a *gendarme* next time?'

'*Non*. I like my soldiers! Please, *mademoiselle*.' Desi reached for his *chasseur* and she saw strikingly his resemblance to his father; the bright and demanding eyes, the mutinous mouth, the eager desire to have what pleased him. 'When I grow up I shall go into the army. I shall be an officer like my grandpapa, with gold braid on my *kepi*.'

He went off to play in the windowseat with his new acquisition, and Margo gave Raoul an inquiring look. 'He means the father of Maxine,' Raoul explained. 'He was a commanding officer in Algeria; a captain of Spahis when a young man, and later, when the war came, he had his own battalion. His blood is in the child, see you? These things assert themselves.'

'But Paul – Paul wishes him to learn the wine business.'

Raoul shrugged his shoulders and spread his hands. 'This is not Paul's child, eh? This is the son of Michel and Maxine.'

'Maxine,' she murmured, and then turned to Desi with a swift smile. '*Mon petit*, we are to go and see your *maman* when I have washed your face and hands and changed your clothes. You will be able to show her your *chasseur*.'

He nodded and slowly smiled ... Michel's son ... who would inherit Satancourt, and perhaps turn away from its turreted beauty and the immaculate grape terraces that hung like evergreen gardens above the silvery waters of the lake.

'Come.' Margo held out her hand to Desi, and tried to wipe from her mind the thought of Paul, whose heart and soul belonged to what was not his.

CHAPTER EIGHT

THE suite of Maxine Cassalis was every bit as lovely as Margo had expected, with deep pale carpeting underfoot, gold silk walls, long sofas covered with turquoise silk, and a collection of exquisite porcelain for the eyes to rest upon.

A harmonious, expensive sitting-room, with a silver lamp shining beside the day-bed on which Maxine rested. She wore a violet-coloured robe with fur around the wide sleeves. She wore her matt-black hair in a straight troubador style, and she was still beautiful in a haunting way, despite the scar on her cheek – white against the olive skin, and shaped curiously like a cross.

She held out a thin hand to Desi, but he didn't run to her with youthful abandon, as he sometimes ran to Margo. He walked quietly, and with a touching dignity he kissed her cheek; the left side that was unmarked and smoothly olive as his own.

'How are you, Maman?' he asked. 'Are you feeling better?'

'I am always better when I see you, my baby.'

He nodded, bit his lip, and then burst out: 'But I am not a baby, Maman. Look, I have a new soldier! Do you like him?'

She looked, and Margo saw the heavy lids close for a moment over her dark, rather slanting eyes. Her hand gripped Desi, until suddenly he pulled away. 'Look, Maman, you dig your fingernails into me!'

'Forgive me, *chéri*. I do it out of love, believe me.' Maxine looked with those haunted eyes at Margo. 'So you are Miss Jones? You must excuse me for not having asked to meet you before, but I am never terribly well, and I did not want you to see Desi's scarred and crippled mother until you had grown fond enough of him not to run away from me. I am glad you are young. Desi needs to be with a young woman. In fact you are quite lovely, Miss Jones. You should be married, with a baby of your own.'

Margo smiled, and her smile quickened as Desi turned his head and gave his mother an eloquent look. 'I have wanted so much to meet you, *madame*. You are every bit as pretty as Desi told me you were, so why should I want to run away from you?'

'Because sad people are boring to the young. You have met Céleste? She is supposed to be living here to keep me company, but the truth is that it is my brother-in-law to whom she likes to give her company. Please sit down – Margo. You don't mind that I call you so? I feel a hundred years older than you, but I suppose we are really the same age. I have lived, and died, but you are poised on the rim of life, waiting to be swept into the passion and pain of it by a man. It is terrifying, when all is said and done, that a single man has the illimitable power to bring out the stars for a woman, or turn them dark.'

Margo sat down on a velvet love-seat, and the thought stole in and out of her mind that Michel might sometimes have occupied this seat, in which lovers could sit and yet be kept apart. Desi had laid himself down on a white rug, and propped on his elbow he was gazing intently at his mother's face. He had often whispered into Margo's ear that his mother was very pretty, except for a mark on her face.

It was symbolic, that little scar. And fascinating, thought Margo. If this young and tragic woman had not loved Michel so blindly, so that she clung to her invalid chair and her solitude, she would surely excite the imagination and the emotions of another man. She was sensitive rather than timid, Margo decided. She would have clothed Michel in fine shining armour; loved him for his handsome face and his persuasive charm. If rumours ever crept to the edges of her heaven, she would have scorned them.

Michel had made the stars shine for her, and that was love, and it cancelled out all the faults and all the little failings, and it intensified the sadness of Maxine's statement that she had lived, and died.

'You are a success with my son,' she went on. 'Are you a success with other members of the family? It is not exactly a gentle family, is it? Old, proud, and fiery, but not gentle. When I came to Satancourt as a bride I was a little afraid of Michel's mother. I wanted to please her, but all she really wanted was that I do my duty by Michel. Then there was Paul. I remember when I was introduced to him, all I could do was hold tightly to Michel's arm, and Paul must have thought me such a fool of a girl. It was harvest time, you see. He was almost black from the sun, and there were wine stains all over his shirt, and he was wearing clogs like a peasant. I was a little snob of a fool then. I didn't know until the day I fainted at his feet and he carried me up all those steps from the gazebo that he had great gentleness and the shocking wisdom of the man who has toiled side by side with his workers. Michel was absent at that time, travelling for Paul on the Côte d'Or. The weather was hot and troubled, and I was to have my child, so I thought, in two months' time. But Paul knew I would have it that day. Such a terrible day! A storm broke and half the vines were torn down in the *mistral*. A boat could not be taken across the lake to bring a doctor. Word could not be sent to Michel because we were unsure of his exact whereabouts. I might have died had it not been for Paul, and the sun-gnarled grape-picker whom he brought to my bedroom. Between them they brought Desi into the world, and Paul breathed into his tiny mouth until he was strong enough to breathe for himself.'

Maxine sat a moment, gazing at her wedding ring, encircled by a band of softly gleaming rubies. 'I was always a dreaming kind of girl, and Michel was my only lover. It was days before I could really look at Paul and thank him for what he had done. He smiled – there is a certain smile that belongs only to Paul. Nothing on earth could ever embarrass him, and he was amused, so greatly amused that I should be embarrassed. He took my hand – this left hand that bears his brother's ring – and he carried it to his lips and kissed it, without speaking. Michel I loved, but in that moment I knew what it felt like to come face to face with a *grand seigneur*. I wonder sometimes if he will marry Céleste. I hope for this. She is a pretty thing. She would be good for him. Someone for him to come home to. And yet, for him, would she be enough – enough of a battle?'

The young widow looked at Margo, so unaware that Margo had known her husband, and had already been drawn into a strange, tense relationship with Paul. 'I think if I suggested to Paul that he marry Céleste, just to please me, he might do it. Do you think I would be wrong to do this? I know she is but a girl, but a girl soon becomes a woman – ah, you look at me with rather shocked eyes, Margo. You think I should not interfere in the matter?'

'If they care for each other, *madame*, it will happen naturally.'

'Being British you take the view that marriages should not be arranged?'

'I suppose I do take that view, *madame*.'

'You are a romantic, and it would very much please me if you would call me Maxine. We are so close in age, and you are not the usual flighty sort of girl one has to deal with.'

'Did you think I might be?' Margo smiled a little. 'I mean, when you heard that I was quite young?'

'The thought did cross my mind,' Maxine confessed. 'There was another girl here about a year ago, and I think the isolation must have turned her head. She used to go up to the grape terraces and one of the men – anyway, she was pulled out of the lake, hysterical, and she accused Paul of being responsible for her trouble. We all knew the idea was ridiculous. Paul had never looked at her. But mud when thrown has a tendency to cling, so I hope you have not been misled by any of the rumours you may have heard?'

Margo shook her head and thought it best not to mention the way Yvonne Dalbert had tried to mislead her. She glanced around the *boudoir* and said admiringly: 'You have a very beautiful room, *madame*. But I never see you in the gardens, which are also beautiful, and I wondered if one day you might come for a small outing with Desi and myself?'

At once a closed expression came over Maxine's face. 'I cannot walk, and I prefer to keep to my rooms. I have my veranda and catch some air from there.'

'But it would give Desi such pleasure, would it not, *mon petit*?' Margo glanced down at him, but he had fallen asleep on the white rug, his lashes in dark crescents against his cheeks. 'He loves you dearly and talks of you so often.'

'I – I have no desire to be part of the world beyond these doors. I have all that I require, all that I could possibly want, for an invalid.'

'If only you would make the effort to go beyond those doors – there is still so much for you to enjoy. You are young, and lovely—'

'Have you not seen this?' Maxine touched her cheek. 'I was wearing a crucifix which Michel had brought back for me from one of his trips, and it was set with tiny diamonds. When the engine of his boat exploded the crucifix was flung up against my face and it embedded itself. Did you know that? It is all I have that is part of that day. My clothes were torn from me and I was flung into the water. Michel – my poor Michel was not so lucky. I cannot – I won't come back to life without him! He was my life, and you wouldn't understand that. You are not in love. Your eyes alone tell me that you have never really loved because you have never really suffered. You are attractive, so there have been men, but nothing so far *sérieux*. I will tell you frankly that my marriage was arranged for me, but from the moment I saw Michel I loved him. He had such grace, such charm, such a way with him. In some ways I was timid and not like Céleste, but he was never impatient with me. You say the gardens of the chateau are beautiful, and who knows it better than I, who have walked in them so often while I waited for Michel to return from these trips he had to make in connection with the business. There is the gazebo by the lake – how often have I sat in there, a book idle beside me as I sat and gazed at the lake – never dreaming that one day—'

Maxine broke off and clenched her hands so tightly together that her ruby ring must have dug into her flesh. 'I cannot walk, and they say it is the shock. Such a shock will last while I live, so I will never walk, or run, or dance again. What have I to dance for? Who have I to run to greet?'

'Your boy,' Margo said gently. 'You say you have nothing left of Michel, but look down there, on the rug fast asleep. There you have his son.'

'I have more or less given him to Paul,' Maxine said, in a remote voice. 'Paul will train him to run the business when the time comes. It is better for him to be with a man more often than he is with a woman whose heart ran out of her with the blood that ran from her face. You must see the wisdom of that, Margo?'

'In a way,' Margo admitted. 'There must be a man in

the boy's life for him to look up to, but you are young, Maxine. You cannot think of your emotional life as being over. In time you might love again—'

'Never! And who would want me? A woman in a wheelchair, with a marked face?' Even as Maxine asked these questions there came a knock at her door and her words hung in the air as the door opened and Raoul d'Arcy presented himself.

He had changed his suit for a dark blue polo-shirt and grey slacks cut narrowly and with slant pockets. He looked attractive and virile, and less casual than his clothes made him appear. 'I shall make a swift disappearance if I am in the way,' he said. 'But I heard you had visitors and I thought I would join the party. May I come in, Maxine?'

'You seem already to be in,' she said drily. 'How are you, Raoul? Still breaking hearts along the boulevards of Paris?'

'How unkind women are to me! They never take me seriously for one moment.' He came to Maxine, took both her hands and kissed each one in turn; real kisses, Margo noticed, and not the usual gallant pantomime that passed for hand-kissing in France. He looked steadily at the upraised, pansy-eyed face. 'You still have the advantage of the gay ladies I meet in Paris, my dear. They dance and drink all night and they make the House of Arden richer by the moment. It is most refreshing to come to the *iles* and find two young women as fresh as if dipped in ice-water. What it does for a man is only comparable to what a dip in the ocean does on a hot, tiring day.'

'I gather, *mon ami*, that Paris is hot and noisy with traffic?'

'Indeed. I thought of being here, of stepping ashore among the willows and seeing the turrets so aloof and untouchable, and so quiet; and so I came, bag and tools, and here I am, *chère amie*. You are pleased to see me?'

Maxine studied him in turn before replying, and Margo wondered if that lean charm of d'Arcy's reminded the young widow of her husband. Margo thought it possible, and she wondered why he had been prowling around the gazebo which had once been such a haunt of Maxine's.

'It is always nice to see old friends,' she said to him. 'Have you had your tea?'

'Miss Jones was kind enough to give me a cup. What a lucky chap is Desi to have for his own private *bonne* such a delectable young woman. I envy him.'

'You always had an eye for the young women, Raoul.'

'True. I have often given them my eye, but I have kept my heart for only one woman.'

'I can't quite believe that you could ever be faithful to one woman, Raoul. Your artistic eye would always see something to admire in someone else, and your wife would have to endure this, or leave you. Endurance wears out in time, you know. The well runs dry. You do best to stay a bachelor.'

'But if I don't marry I shall end up a lonely old man,' he said, with a mock self-pity which seemed to Margo to hold elements of the truth. Confirmed bachelors were either men who disliked women or those who liked every woman. Raoul struck her as a charmer but not as a Casanova.

'Marriage is no real cure for loneliness,' said Maxine thoughtfully. 'Only love can fill the heart and make life thoroughly worthwhile. You must fall in love, *mon cher.*'

'That is just the trouble, I am in love,' he said quietly.

'Then what is to stop you from marrying the girl?'

'The girl herself. If I dared to tell her how I feel she would tell me to stay away from her. I am caught in a trap, you see. I want to share my life with her, but if I told her so then she would refuse to share another moment with me. She prefers my friendship. She has no time for my passion.'

'She sounds a very cold creature, Raoul. You would do better to forget all about her.'

'But that is the trouble with love, Maxine. It grips and won't let go. It is everything in one person, heaven and hell, and I can no more forget my love than you—' He broke off, looked at Desi, glanced at the darkening windows, and seemed deeply disturbed. 'You know what love is, Maxine. I don't have to explain it to you, of all people. *Mon Dieu*, who has been more hurt by it than you!'

'Hurt?' She took up the word quickly, even as Margo was bracing herself to leave these two in discussion while she took Desi to bed. The sharp note in Maxine's voice made her eyes go quickly to the oval, pale-olive face, marked by the crucifix which Michel had given her. She was sitting forward, staring at Raoul. 'What do you mean when you say that?' she demanded of him. 'I had happiness with Michel. I had all that I asked of him. I *loved* him.'

'And he loved himself with equal devotion.'

First came the words, swift and inevitable, somehow. And then came the sound of the slap as Maxine raised her hand and struck Raoul across the face. And as she did so she moved her legs so as to bring herself closer to him, to hit him all the harder. And after the slap came the sound of her choked sob.

'Your legs – did you see?' Raoul gripped her, held her, and seemed uncaring of the blow she had dealt him. '*Chérie*, did you feel them move?'

'I – I did move,' she said. 'Raoul, you made me so angry—'

'You may be a thousand times more angrier if it will do

the trick and bring you back to life!' He looked exultant, and as Margo rose to her feet she was in no doubt as to the woman he was in love with. It was a love which must have started while Maxine was married to Michel, and it was a good love if this virile and life-loving man had not been put off by Maxine's inability to walk and to face up to being a woman again, with a woman's hopes and desires.

Margo quietly aroused the sleepy boy and drew him to his feet. 'Say *bon soir* to your *maman* and to your Uncle Raoul,' she murmured. 'It is time for you to go to bed, *petit.*'

'Maman?' The child stared at his mother as if something in her face struck him as different, and strange.

'*Chéri*, come kiss me good night.' She held open her arms and Desi ran into them and he hugged her with sudden fearlessly loving arms.

Margo didn't dare to look at Raoul. It would be almost an intrusion into his private hopes and fears. Even if Maxine recovered the use of her limbs she might never recover the will to love another man ... of course none of them could be in any more doubt that she had known of Michel's lack of faithfulness ... that was why she had slapped Raoul. To hear him speak of it, to have it put into words, had hurt her so much that she had needed to hurt him in return.

'*Bon soir, bon soldat.*' Raoul and Desi solemnly saluted each other. 'You take heed of Mademoiselle and you will grow up to be a real man.'

They went off to the nursery suite and left Maxine alone with Raoul. Perhaps he would stay and dine with her; on the veranda would be nice, as it was a warm, soft night. Having broken through her defences it was up to Raoul not to retreat again, not to give in to his fear of losing half his cake for the sake of wanting the whole confection ... the big brown eyes, the hair like heavy mourning silk, and the sad heart that only a sincere love could ever hope to make joyous.

Margo had tucked Desi into his bed and she was telling him a story when she caught the soft burring sound of the house telephone in the adjoining room.

She left the story in mid-air and went to answer the call. A deep voice struck against her eardrum. 'Is that Miss Jones?'

'Yes, *m'sieur*.' She stared at the nursery wallpaper, with its nymphs and gnomes scampering among woodland trees, and felt the sudden nervous beating of her heart. 'Have you dialled the wrong number?'

'I think not. I am going up to the terraces – there is a full moon and they are quite a picture by moonlight. You have not really seen them as it is too hot up there during the daytime and I wondered if you would like to come with me? We can take some food with us and a bottle of the *rosé*. Anyway, think about it. I can tell by your breathless silence that you are preparing to say no, and it is such a puritanical little word, and should be dismissed from the mind on a night of the Bacchus moon. If you decide to dismiss that tiny spoil-sport of a word, then I shall be waiting on the lakeside path that leads to the terraces in exactly one hour from now.'

There was a click and the telephone was dead against her ear. She lowered the receiver and stared at it tongue-bound. She knew he was daring her to do this mad thing out of sheer devilment. She pictured him at the other end of the line, a sardonic smile on his mouth as he regarded the telephone and waited for it to buzz an angry answer at him. She was almost tempted to dial his study and to say coldly that she was not interested in seeing his precious vines by moonlight . . . only it wouldn't be true.

She knew when she had left Maxine alone with Raoul that a wistful desire for romance had stirred in her heart. She had been deeply touched that a man could love like

146

that, so gallantly and unselfishly. She cradled the receiver and knew that Paul was offering not love but a duel of the senses; a flight into danger.

'*Mademoiselle* ...?'

Desi was calling her and she returned to finish his bedtime story, and when his eyes had closed and his breathing told her that he was fast asleep, she brushed a kiss across his forehead and quietly left his room. She made her thoughtful way along the carpeted corridor to the stairs that led to the upper landing, and as she approached her rooms she could see the moon shining beyond the window at the end of the corridor. It was so bright as to be silver, and immensely attractive as it swung there against the velvety grey of the sky. A fool's moon ... a lover's moon ... a devil's moon.

Margo stood gazing at it for a long moment, and weighed dinner in the company of Madame Cassalis and her companion against that of a moonlit picnic with Paul, up there among the grape-hung vines, the great clusters of wine berries that stretched their skins each day in the hot sun until when they were almost at bursting point they would be swooped upon by the grape-pickers, cut from the vines and piled into the wide-brimmed head baskets, which in their turn would be emptied into the oxen carts and taken to the mill to be crushed not by the pounding feet any longer but by the modern machinery installed to do the work so much faster if not so romantically.

She glanced at her wristwatch and saw that twenty minutes of the hour had gone and that if she was going to take up the gauntlet which Paul had thrown down, then she had better make haste – while the moon shone!

She took a shower and enjoyed the cool pelting of the water against her skin. Sarong-wrapped by her bathtowel, she opened the deep cupboard which was tangy with lavender, the heads of which were scattered all over the floor of the closet, so that over the years the oil from the lavender had penetrated the wood and made it a place of incense. Margo could step right into the closet, it was so large, and she always had the feeling that in days gone by a lover could have been concealed in it, among the silk flounces and long velvet skirts, grinding his heels in the lavender as the door enclosed him in darkness, feeling sure his heartbeats could be heard through the door as his mistress argued, perhaps, with a stern and arrogant husband.

Smiling a little, as she always did at this flight of fancy, Margo took a dress of finely pleated silk from its hanger, a pale lily colour that so enhanced her hair that she never dared to wear the dress in front of Madame Cassalis.

She didn't dare to question her own motive in wearing it to meet Paul on that path to moonlight madness. She slid it down over her body and cinched the narrow belt of silver. She was crazy, she told herself again. This was a dress to be worn with cocktails and irrelevant conversation in a cab driving to a smart supper club where the orchestra would play dreamy dance music.

Up there on the terraces they would drink that dark-rose wine and the only orchestra would be the thousands of cicadas hidden in the foliage of the trees.

Margo held the long swathe of her hair away from her face and she saw in the mirror how defiantly blue were her eyes. Then she swathed her hair to the crown of her head, leaving bare her slender neck as if for the sword of Damocles. She fixed her hair with a circular pin that glittered with tiny bright stones, and she wondered what earthly excuse she would make to Madame Cassalis if she should run into her on the stairs or down in the hall. Margo glanced at her watch and reckoned that if she hurried away now she would just about avoid Madame on her way to the *salon* for her aperitif, a slender glass of very dry sherry. But just to be on the safe side Margo snatched a coat from her closet and belted it. Her dress was knee-length so it didn't show, and if she met the inquisitive Yvonne she could always say that she was snatching a breath of air. She had no idea what excuse Paul had made about not joining his mother for dinner, but she felt pretty sure he had covered his tracks. He wouldn't arrange this moonlight picnic without ensuring secrecy, and Margo had already found out that he and the *chef* Hercule were very good friends. The basket of food would be supplied without any indiscreet questions being asked, and Paul would select the wine himself.

Margo sped down the three flights of stairs, wide and gracefully balustraded with wrought-iron, so that her fleeing figure in an English tweed coat was slightly incongruous. With her heart beating fast like a caged bird whose door had been mischievously opened she flew across the hall and along the cool covered way to the courtyard. The moon was riding high over the chateau and the lake and the whole garden was soft with petals, green and purple and sensuous. She saw a cluster of small roses all open in the moonlight as if they were fooled and thought the sun was glowing instead of a huge crystal ball just made for broomstick flying, or the telling of fortunes.

Margo reached the gate in the fuchsia hedges where the ballerina flowers were so detailed by the moonlight that they seemed to dance as she pushed open the gate that led in the direction of the lake. There she paused for a moment and gazed at the moon as if for guidance. She could still turn back to the edgy security of the usual sort of evening, seated across the table from Yvonne, with Madame Cassilis facing her son's empty chair. The well-cooked food would be brought quietly and at regular intervals to the table, and Yvonne would give Margo an insolent stare whenever Madame's attention was upon her food.

Suddenly a bird chirped at the moon, and Margo con-

tinued on her way along the stone border of the garden.
'*C'est la vie!*' she murmured, and tall velvety hollyhocks
brushed her hair as they stood sentinel at the top of the
steps leading down to the lake. There were statues half-
way down where the steps branched and they looked so
ghostly that Margo was glad when she reached the
ground and stood on the path that ran beside the lake.

The water of the lake was aglow with ripples and swirls
of silver; the tips of the reeds glinted like swords upended
on their hilts, and the willows hung their mad green
tresses to the ground and made a whispering sound as a
soft breeze stirred across the water and brushed Margo's
face.

Paul had said that he would be waiting on the path for
her, and she thrust her hands into the pockets of her coat
and did not hurry towards the bend in the path, where
the ground took a gradual rise and wended its way
upwards, until it was lost among the hanging vines.

As she drew nearer to the bend she could hear someone
softly whistling and she recognized the music of the tenor
song *La Donna è Mobile*. Her hands clenched in her
pockets and she told herself that when she came face to
face with Paul she would tell him that she had changed
her mind about wining and dining with him among his
grapevines. Did he imagine that she had no choice but to
come to him? That she answered some sort of primitive
call and had no will of her own?

She rounded the bend, but the words on her lips took
the form of a startled gasp. He was seated on the back of
his black horse, the reins slack in his hand as he whistled
softly and the sound was carried across the silver silence
of the lake. His hair, his white shirt, and the coat of his
mount were sheened by the moonlight, and when he
glanced from the water to Margo the silvery light was
turned to mercury in his eyes and she knew for certain
that she must go back to the chateau and not chance

being alone with him.

'So there you are! And you are five minutes late and lucky that I waited for you.'

'I came to tell you – I am not coming with you to the terraces!'

'Little liar.' He whispered the words and yet they stung as if the tip of a lash sped across her skin. 'You didn't need to come at all to let me know you were not interested in a moonlight picnic. You could have gone sedately into dinner with Maman, but your curiosity, and your sense of adventure, swayed you in my direction. Are you going to turn coward now you have come this far?'

'It – wasn't until I was half-way here that I realized how odd it would look if both of us – if you and I failed to appear for dinner.'

'My absence is due to pressure of work in my study, and orders have been issued that I am not to be disturbed – at any cost. I actually locked the door on the inside and left by the window.' A slow smile lit his teeth against his dark face. 'Such lavish precautions are slightly ridiculous, are they not? That you and I can't take an hour or two together without danger to your reputation? I am glad to see that you are not in uniform – or are you wearing it under that coat?'

'Of course not – I mean, *m'sieur*, you know very well that I always change for dinner.'

'And you know very well, *mademoiselle*, that you didn't come this far in order to tell me that you prefer to dine under my mother's eye. I have watched you, so outwardly polite and sedate, and so full of inward rebellion. The ritual of the serving of the food in splendid silence and each one of us seated in a hard-backed chair with an island of cutlery and plate in front of us. You long for a relaxation of these age-old rules and rituals, don't you? You would like to hear laughter at the table, and afterwards you would like music to be played in the *salon* and all business talk banished for the evening. Well, *mademoiselle*, am I wrong about you, or am I right?'

She stared at him and could not tell from his face whether he approved her wishes or thought them highly impudent in a mere governess. Even Céleste preferred to dine with her sister rather than under the stern gaze of Madame, for there was no chance to flirt with Paul while his mother looked on.

Margo's heart gave a little jolt. Was it his intention to flirt with *her* away from the cool watching eyes ... the eyes that long ago had gaily laughed and dared recklessly to love a young man who worked for her father and whom she would never have been allowed to marry. Had they run away together the arms of parental influence would have reached out to bring her back ... in disgrace. So she had chosen to conduct her love affair in secret, and that compulsion was in Paul's blood.

Margo backed away from him. 'I am going back to the house, *m'sieur*. I was a fool to come here—'

'Why?' he demanded, and his hand tightened on the reins and the black horse shifted his position. 'Because suddenly you see the invitation in the light of a seduction? I thought we established the fact that you find me less attractive than you found my brother?'

'Why ask me to eat supper with you upon the terraces?' she asked. 'Why *me* when there is Céleste and she – well, she makes no secret of the fact that she likes you.'

'Céleste is little more than a child, *mademoiselle*. She amuses me, but I would never dream of making advances to her.'

'But I am in a different position,' Margo shot back at him. 'I am employed here and so you think I am at your beck and call. I am going back – I can always say that I went out for some air and lost track of the time.'

As she turned away and started to walk along the path, the hooves of the horse suddenly quickened behind her and Paul cantered in front of her and barred her way to the chateau. He sat there above her, outlined by the moon, and adamant as a figure carved in stone. 'You are coming with me, *mademoiselle*. I offered you escape from that restricting dining-room for this one night when the moon will reveal every grape on the vine as if it were a gem. I don't care to have such an offer flung back in my face! Now give me your hand and step on to my boot, and don't be nervous of Sable. His temper is really much better than mine.'

She was quite sure that his temper was impetuous and ruthless ... she saw it sparking in his eyes, felt it in the flexing of his fingers as his hand reached down and had hold of hers before she even realized that she had raised it.

'My boot will take your weight – come, Miss Jones.'

Now that he had hold of her hand it was useless to argue with him, so she did as he ordered and felt herself lifted into the saddle in front of him, and was very much aware of the strength that lay in his shoulders and in his features.

'Are you quite comfortable?' he drawled above her head. 'If you will relax and not sit like a poker you will enjoy the ride very much more.'

It was impossible to relax! To have done so would have brought her at rest against his broad chest, which she knew to be bare under his shirt. 'I am all right,' she said, and felt the nervous beating of her heart as his arms encircled her in order to hold the reins and direct his mount. He backed Sable into the bend where he would have more room to turn around, and then they were cantering up the slope of the path, and Margo gripped the front of the saddle in order not to be thrown back against Paul. She was so acutely aware of his closeness that it was like a very refined form of torture.

Knowing his brother had not taught her that there

were wilder shores of physical emotion than those of dancing to soft music with an attractive man who had charm at his fingertips.

There had been no peril in sharing a moonlit terrace with Michel ... but here among the tumbling vines the very air she breathed held a dangerous intoxication. Sable was strong and he seemed not to mind the double burden as the slope grew steeper, until suddenly it branched beneath the spread sails of the windmill and they came out upon a plateau above the lake itself, a sort of stone hoop that held the terraces like the wide frills of a crinoline skirt.

The whole effect was amazingly dramatic and beautiful, so that as Sable stood there huffing his nostrils, and they sat there just looking, and breathing it all, it was almost like a dream. Nothing so breathtaking could be real, and then Paul spoke:

'You will never forget this moment,' he said. 'No matter what has gone before in your life, no matter what comes after, the drama of this place will never be erased for you.'

CHAPTER NINE

MARGO sat very still in his arms, and everything else seemed still until he spoke again. The world moved once more and she was aware of the whispering vines and the soft coolness of the air against her skin.

'In the distant past, when people believed in the magic and the sorcery of things, this was said to be a place of enchantment and at the full of the moon the spirit of the wine god was set free and magic was distilled into the grapes of Satancourt.' Paul glanced down at her; she couldn't see his eyes but she felt his gaze on her hair. 'When you are far away in some other place, the memory of all this will return to you at an unexpected moment. Then, perhaps, you will understand why I stay here. Why I allow myself to be a prisoner of love of something which is not really mine.'

He swept out a hand and the rose-crest engraved ring caught the moonlight and gleamed black and gold. 'When a boy I used to come up here to join in the harvesting of the grapes and the treading of the wine. I would crumble the black earth in my fingers and breathe the acids and the sugars on my fingers. I filled my hands with grapes and I crushed them until the juice ran wine red to my very elbows. I believed I was to be the master of all this in due time, and love of it entered too deep into my soul and my bones for me to leave when I learned the truth about myself – that I was not truly a Cassalis. I did run away at first. I worked at other vineyards, but in the end I returned. I was like a gardener who knew that if he stayed away his vineyard would perish.'

As Paul spoke his hand curled around Margo's slim neck and he forced her to turn and look at him. His eyes stared down into hers, as if compelling her to believe his every word. As if for him this moment was strangely significant.

'This is my world, Margo,' he said, and never before had he used her first name, and this too seemed significant. 'It bound my roots to its own before I was ever told that I had no birthright to it – but let me assure you that unlike Cain I did not strike down my brother.'

'Paul – I never believed that you did!'

'No?' His fingers tightened on her nape and they expressed more forcibly than words his disbelief in her protest. 'When you heard that Michel had died, you came here to Satancourt in order to try and protect his son from the wicked uncle – myself!'

'I knew nothing about you,' she protested. 'Michel never mentioned to me that he had a brother and it wasn't until my interview with your mother that I learned of your existence.'

'It was out of mere sentiment that you applied for this post of *bonne* to my young nephew?' Paul spoke cynically. 'All the same it must have come as a shock when you met me. I bear no likeness to Michel, do I?'

'None at all,' she confessed. 'No two brothers could be so unalike.'

'Was the disappointment very acute, Miss Jones?'

'No – why should it be?'

'Ah, you might have hoped to see shades of your old love.' His smile was slightly mocking as he dismounted and held out his arms so that she could reach the ground with his assistance. She wished she could have leapt down and ignored him, but Sable was shifting about now Paul was out of the saddle and the ground looked hard. Bracing herself, she slid down into his arms and felt them close about her body. He gazed down at her face in the moonlight, letting his eyes rove her features as she stood still within the circle of his arms ... aware and striving not to reveal how aware she was of his physical strength and his dark magnetism which had nothing to do with deliberate cultivated charm.

'I am never sure,' he murmured, 'when your face is most appealing, when you smile or when you look at me with such grave and questioning eyes. Must I have a definite reason for wanting you to visit the groves to-night? Can't I now and then be a man of whims – like my brother? Though we never looked alike, Michel and I, we had one or two impulses in common.'

'Why did he never mention you, I wonder?' Margo in her turn studied his face so clearly revealed by the moon-light, the strong planes and bones of it so unlike that other face last seen by the light of another moon. 'Did you and he quarrel, Paul? Was it no longer possible for you to be friends after you learned that he was the heir to all that you cared for most in your life?'

'Am I now vindictive, bitter, and hateful?' he mocked. 'If I judge correctly Michel never gave me a thought with you on his mind. He was always inclined to be bored by the fact that I enjoy work as he enjoyed – women. His gay ways always appealed to them. He knew how to slip in and out of the chains of love – he never really cared for anyone but himself and his own pleasures.'

Margo didn't protest against this, for now she knew it to be the undeniable truth. It had been easy for Michel to leave her on that other moonlit terrace . . . easy for him to take Maxine for his wife, knowing that she loved him too blindly to ever accuse him of infidelity.

Margo sighed, and in that instant Paul turned away from her and took Sable by the reins to be tethered to a tree. The green frogs leapt in the moonlight, and Margo could see the grapes dripping in clusters from the hanging vines. She could smell the rich earth which all day had been fed with the hot sunshine, and behind her was the white-stoned conical tower of the mill, the sails like sleeping batwings in the moonlight. The whole scene had an enchantment she was acutely aware of ... she was unaware of the witchery of her own eyes, so strangely shining as they took in the beauty of the night.

'Come,' said Paul. 'I brought the food and wine up earlier, and everything is ready for us.'

She went with him to where a cane table was laid beside the stone wall that surmounted the terraces. 'Under the trees there are gnats and you don't want to be bitten,' he said. 'Does it strike you as strange to dine in this way?'

'Unusual,' she replied, 'but then you are not a usual sort of man, are you, *m'sieur*?'

'You think not?' The wine cork sighed as he pulled it from the bottle and the glasses sparkled darkly as he filled them. 'I don't have to taste this wine; I know its perfection. There you are, Miss Jones. Wine and chicken, olives and bread. Food of the gods.'

'A while ago you called me Margo.' She held her wine glass by its slender stem, and she watched him as he sat down at the other side of the table, his white shirt gleaming against the sun-darkened skin of his throat and his arms. How broad his shoulders were, as if made to carry burdens that other men would grow desperately tired of. She thought of what Maxine had said, that if he married Céleste he would have someone to give him comfort and ease at the end of his long day. Did he really toil so hard for the sake of Michel's son? Or did some dark and secret flame of hope burn in his soul that one day ... one day what he loved so well might really be his?

His strong hands broke cold roasted chicken ... and a tiny shiver ran through Margo. He looked illimitably the kind of man to get all that he wanted from life, either by strength or sheer determination. He did not waste time on charming a woman, but all the same he had persuaded her to come and dine all alone with him, high above the chateau, where she would be entirely at his mercy if he chose to make love to her.

'You are not eating,' he said. 'Aren't you hungry? Or are you nervous of me?'

'Have I reason to be nervous?' she asked, picking up a chicken leg and taking a bite to show him that her nerves weren't entirely shaken.

'Sitting there in your white dress, cool as a cloister, you are naturally in danger of stirring the imagination of any man – and both of us are all too aware that I am not Michel.'

'Please – must we talk about him?' There was pain in her voice; the awful pain of disillusion, and she quickly reached for her wine and then gave a gasp as she sent the glass toppling over so that the red wine ran like blood all over the checked cloth. 'Oh, dear!' She jumped to her feet, but not in time to avoid a spill of the wine on to the white skirt of her dress. 'How clumsy of me!'

'Indeed.' In a stride he was at her side and proffering a large white handkerchief. 'Try this, but I fear the wine will stain that soft material. Such a pity—'

'It was my own fault – thank you.' She took the handkerchief and dabbed at the wine stains, but they stayed dark against the white chiffon, and with a wry little shrug she dropped the folds back into place. 'They may come out when the dress is cleaned, so don't let's worry about it.'

'You are all on edge, aren't you?' He returned the handkerchief to his pocket, and his brows were drawn down darkly to shade his grey eyes. 'Well, I am going to insist that you drink the next glass of wine and relax from your tension. Really, Miss Jones, one would think that I had it on my mind to take advantage of you, when all I really wanted was a little company.'

He turned from her to refill her glass, and she clutched at the terrace wall and felt that she might fall if she didn't hold on to something solid. Was he really so lonely that he had to turn to her of all people to help him forget for a while that the future of Satancourt depended on a boy who might well turn out to be exactly like his father. It was no use any more for her to make excuses for Michel . . . she had been young, unworldly, when he had charmed his way into her heart. She had clung to the memory of the romance he had brought into her life, but she was learning, painfully, that there was more to loving a man than dancing to sweet music and listening to whispers that were no more than moondust.

Paul held out a fresh glass of wine and she took it very carefully, and she even managed to smile at him. '*Merci, m'sieur.* You must consider it a crime to see good wine wasted?'

'We must all spill a little wine before we really grow up,' he said, and leaned his back against the wall and studied the sky that was moon drowned, so that birds and cicadas and the sea were made restless by that almost supernatural glow. 'Man is like the moon, you know, Margo. He has two sides to him, one in shadow and the other in sunlight.'

'What of women?' she asked. 'Are they the stars?'

'Perhaps so. Scintillating and constant, and when you fall, you fall all the way to earth.'

'With a bump!' she smiled.

He shrugged and his glance touched her face, her hair, the soft material of her dress. His gaze was caught and held by the fine gold chain glinting against her collarbone. His fingers had lightly touched it before she knew his intention, and fine as a thread and yet shocking as fire was the effect the brush of his fingers had on her. She stood almost without breathing as he withdrew from the neck of her dress the tiny cross attached to the chain.

'Protection against the devil?' he murmured.

'Is that what you want to think?' she asked.

'Naturally. I still recall the effect I had on you when I showed you the wine *chai*. It must have taken quite a lot of courage for you to meet me tonight. I mean, what protection would you have against me if I suddenly swept you up in my arms and carried you into the windmill ... apart from the little crucifix? When you fastened it around your neck were you not thinking along those lines? Subconsciously?'

'Chains and charms are merely for adornment, in this day and age,' she said. 'Surely it was only in medieval days that people believed they could be protected against the devil by wearing a cross. I didn't give it a thought—'

'Truly?' He took a step nearer to her. 'Do you really believe that the elemental primitive in man and woman has been tamed to such an extent that we no longer possess basic instincts, only cynical and modern impulses? Sex merely as a satisfaction and not a drive towards another sole individual? Love a dry seed driven on the wind to settle where it will, to take root in any soil, or merely wither away?'

'Aren't we getting off the track – a little?' She moved delicately, as a cat does, out of reach of his hand. 'What has love to do with the devil?'

'What indeed, *ma belle*?' There was something indulgently derisive about his smile. 'Come, we are not eating the good food which I took so much trouble to filch from Hercule's kitchen. Are you not hungry? The wine will go to your head if you don't eat – and that will be very dangerous for you. The moon and the wine might make you amorous.'

'Don't hope for that, Paul.' She could feel her inward defiance of the mixed emotions he aroused with the moonlight on his strong dark face that masked a man who was always a little out of reach even when he was close to her in a physical sense. Her eyes skimmed that black scrolled hair at his temples ... defiance, consternation, the desire to run and yet to remain were racing through her veins. She caught her breath as the long sweet notes of a nightingale echoed from the wine terraces, and she breathed the fragrance of honeysuckle which overhung the wall where they stood and also clustered all down the side of the windmill that during the day was exposed to the sun.

Everything was too evocative tonight, and the only escape was to return to the table and the food. They, at least, were down-to-earth things, and it wouldn't do for the wine to go to her head.

Paul followed her to the table, and they ate goose liver *paté*, small rolled fishes and spiced pickle, and hunks of French bread heaped with the butter and cheese which Hercule made so deliciously in old-fashioned churns.

'Picnics remind me of my boyhood.' Paul lounged back in his chair and lit one of his cheroots, the smoke drifting in an enjoyable stream from his nostrils. 'Strangely enough I enjoyed my young days. He was good to me, the man whom I believed to be my father – the man who believed me to be his son. If Maman had burned that letter to her lover then things need never have changed.'

'I think you know in your heart, Paul, that it was only fair that Michel inherited what was rightfully his.' Margo watched the play of the smoke about Paul's rugged, almost Roman head. 'It isn't as if you were banished from Satancourt. Each day you are here. Each day you see what you love—'

'To love and not to possess can do cruel things to a man, *ma belle*. And you would be on Michel's side in this – it is only natural.'

'Natural?' She took him up quickly. 'Why do you say that?'

'You loved him, did you not? Still love him, perhaps.

Why else would you come here – ready to slay the dragon, but also curious about Michel's family, and his wife in particular. What is your impression of Maxine? I believe you have now seen her and conversed with her?'

'Yes – I liked her. I found her very lovely, and sad. It would be a pity if she allowed her life to be overshadowed by that tragic thing that happened. She has Desi, and—' Margo broke off, for she had been about to mention Raoul d'Arcy and what he felt for Maxine. 'And life must go on no matter how we suffer, one way or another.'

'Indeed. Life is very tenacious, and demanding, and as you say Maxine is rather lovely. Victor Hugo once wrote that the supreme happiness of life is the conviction of being loved for yourself. Therefore the supreme sadness for Maxine must be the knowledge that she was not loved for herself. Tell me, Miss Jones,' Paul leaned forward a little and his eyes held Margo as firmly as if he manually gripped her, 'did my brother give to you the passion he did not give to his wife?'

'I – I took nothing away from Maxine!' Pain and anger flared in Margo's eyes, and in her body. 'How dare you say such a thing? How dare you even think it! After Michel married her, I never saw him again. He went out of my life and I never tried to see him again. I read of his marriage and I left the south of France and returned to my own country.' Suddenly Margo jumped to her feet, hurt by Paul and obeying a blind impulse to get away from his harshness. 'If you're curious to know if Michel was my lover, then you can stay curious, *m'sieur*. I don't owe you any information about my private life; all that is required from me is that I do my work to the satisfaction of Madame Cassalis. I don't have to tolerate your inquisition – your insults – or your damned envy of Michel!'

So saying, she turned to leave him ... and gave a shocked cry of protest when he caught hold of her and swung her to face him. He caught her to him and his face was savage as the light of the moon struck it ... and what was even more terrible for Margo was the wild thrill of pleasure that shafted her at the pain of his touch. At once, instinctively, wildly, she had to fight against the feeling and against him.

'You're a brute!' she flung at him. 'I hate and despise you – I believe you would do anything – anything to get what you want!'

'How well your instincts know me,' he mocked, and even as his arms were bruising her, they were welding her to the hard warmth of his body and it was as if his strength was sapping the fight out of her and inducing her to surrender to him despite herself. He had forced her head back against his arm and his eyes dwelt on her lips that called him a brute ... his eyes raked her face as his fingers raked her hair and loosened it.

'Do your instincts also tell you that I want you?' he asked, and his breath was warm against her face. 'How many women do you think there have been while I have been giving all my days and my nights to these terraces? How often do you think I have kissed, and been kissed? I might envy Michel his conquest of you – *mon Dieu*, I might do that, but I won't have you accuse me of any other envy of that – that reckless fool who took that poor girl Maxine for a ride from the moment he married her – until finally he almost killed her! Envy him? For saying that, *ma belle*, I will blot him out from your mind and your senses as if he had never been in them!'

Paul had kissed her before ... but not like this. With a deliberate, sensuous violence that numbed her lips and then brought them achingly alive to every demanding pressure applied to them ... deep, then deeper, until the torment would have been to be wrenched apart from him rather than welded to the bone and muscle and mouth of him.

It was he – he who broke the embrace – tearing his mouth from hers, dragging his arm from around her body, his fingers from her hair, and as if she were suddenly hateful to him he thrust her away from him so that she struck herself against a tree and felt the blow with such acuteness that tears sprang to her eyes. She gave him one look and then fled like a mad thing, guided by the moon down the wide-stepped terraces, and aware that she ran not only from him but from herself.

It seemed ages before she reached ground level, and by then she was so out of breath that she sought shelter in the gazebo and sat down on the iron seat to recover not only her breath but her senses.

If she had ever thought that she loved Michel Cassalis, she knew now that it had been but a chimera; the first awakening of a young girl in a foreign land meeting for the first time a young man of practised charm. It was fled, gone like a puff of smoke, and what had taken its place was a torment of the heart, a tumult of the body, a crying protest against the terrible, unwilling ecstasy of it.

She had fallen in love with a devil in chains . . . a man imprisoned by his love of Satancourt. She had heard him say that he wanted her . . . she knew that she would never hear him say that he loved her.

She stayed alone in the gazebo for about an hour, sensing that he would not come here after thrusting her away from him in that hurtful way. He had meant to hurt her . . . he couldn't know that he had set her heart aching with a strange, hopeless. reluctant love of him.

In the week that followed Margo saw hardly anything of Paul. The moon waned, but not the feelings he had aroused up there among the vines, where the air was so heady as to be almost heathen. The long hot days ripened the grapes and he went off to attend to business on the mainland. Madame Cassalis said he had wine merchants to see, and it was at once a relief to Margo and a curious source of depression not to catch a glimpse of Paul about the estate; nor to see him at the dining-table in the evenings, now grown so warm and long and languorous that a table was set on the outside gallery and the evening meal was served there, to the hidden hum and chirr of the thousands of cicadas that lived their secretive lives in the rich foliage that hung motionless in the warm, dark blue air.

During the day she was mostly with Desi, and sometimes Raoul would join them. He took them boating on the lake, and they moored on one of the tiny islands and there he sketched the boy, and also did a sketch of Margo's head. 'From the start you struck me as attractive,' he told her. 'But suddenly you have a strange new beauty, a depth to your glance, a secret sort of longing in the shape of your lips. Has Satancourt cast a spell over you, I wonder? Is the place bringing out the sorceress in you?'

'Has it that kind of reputation?' she asked, casually at rest on the rock where he had placed her, while Desi hunted in the rock pools for shells and coloured stones. Within herself Margo was recalling vividly what Paul had said about Satancourt . . . that in days gone by it had been thought to be a place of enchantment. 'The name would suggest, Raoul, that it is not always a lucky place.'

'You think Satan had his court here . . . that he might still have it?' Raoul paused in his sketching and studied her not with the eye of an artist but with a glint of anxiety in the expression of his eyes. 'Do you feel something ominous in the atmosphere?' he asked. 'Do you feel that the chateau may be overshadowed by something—' He broke off and gestured at the child. 'I think you have guessed how I feel about him and his mother. I should like to take them away with me, but she – she clings to the idea that she was really happy with her husband. She knows in her heart that it wasn't so, but she wants to believe that he loved her. The poor girl has not yet known love as she deserves to know it!'

Raoul bent his head once more to his sketching and Margo found herself wildly hoping that he would find a way to have Maxine for his own. He would be so good for her . . . and far away in Paris where he had his apartment she would learn to forget the way her marriage had ended.

Now that the ice had been broken between Maxine and herself, she went often to the lovely blue and gold suite to keep the young widow company. Céléste had her own pursuits . . . and Margo knew she was often in Paul's company. Sometimes she would return to the chateau with excited eyes, her dark hair loosened on the shoulders of her silk riding-shirt, giving the impression she had been kissed while alone with Paul. She made no secret of how she felt about him, but there was no telling from his manner, now he had returned from his business trip and resumed his place at the table for meals, how he regarded the girl. His teasing could hide male interest, or mere affection for a young and pretty girl.

Margo only knew that he deeply disturbed her own inner self when he appeared on the roof patio, so vitally dark in his riding breeches and kneeboots latched around the strong thrust of his legs. The sun up on the terraces was tanning his skin so darkly that he looked, she thought, when he descended to the chateau, like a pagan sprung from the wine-dark earth himself.

'Bonjour, mademoiselle,' he drawled, pressing Desi's shoulder with a brown hand as he passed the table and paused beside the peach trellis to select one to eat with his breakfast. 'And where is Céléste this fine morning, eh?

She is usually up and about by now?'

'I believe she had a letter from her father, *m'sieur*. Jean brought it across by boat and something in it seemed to upset her, for she passed me on her way to Maxine's room, and she looked – stormy.'

'I see.' Paul sat down and helped himself to crisp bacon and truffle, and broke bread in hands that made her stare at the deep scratches marking them. He had been in the *chai* all day yesterday, assisting with the cleaning out of the barrels, and she wondered again why he worked until he almost exhausted himself. It was as if – as if he had something on his mind which he needed to forget and work was a more potent palliative than anything else.

'I have an idea,' he said, 'that her father wishes her to return home for a while. He has married again – he was a widower – and Céleste has so far refused to live in the same house with the second wife. She is young, wilful, and wants her own way, of course. I believe you once said that your own mother remarried after the death of your father, *mademoiselle?*'

'Yes – it is always a little awkward to adjust to such a situation, especially when you are no longer a child. I took a job away from home, and I found it was better for my mother not to have me living under the same roof. I – I loved my father rather a lot.'

Paul glanced up from his plate and looked directly at her. 'I think you might have been a little like Céleste at her age – not exactly to look at, but in your ways. You would advise me to let her stay at Satancourt? Not insist that she return home if only for a while?'

It shook Margo a little that he assumed personal charge of Céleste, and she tried not to hate the thought of any girl or woman meaning more to him than she did. 'She is of an age to make her own decisions, *m'sieur*. If she were forced to go home, she would resent her stepmother even more. In time she will come to terms with the situation and realize that her father has feelings like other men and finds loneliness hard to endure.'

'You think, *mademoiselle*, that loneliness is harder for men than for women?' he asked, handing Desi a chunk of bread and butter with truffle on it. The boy gnawed the bread and gazed at Paul's face with the intent eyes of total trust and affection. Margo's fingers clenched her napkin, for if Raoul should ever persuade Maxine to go to Paris with him, then the boy would go with them and she could no longer believe that Paul felt anything but love for the child. If Desi were taken away from him, then he would indeed be lonely . . . unless he married Céleste.

'Women seem to fend better than men,' she replied, 'when it comes to domesticity. But I expect their inner loneliness is just as great if—' She broke off and reached for the coffee pot, aware of Paul's grey eyes glinting across the table at her.

'If love passes them by?' He held out his own cup for a second helping. 'That is what you were about to say, eh?'

'I suppose so.' She gripped the pot tightly, afraid that it might shake in her hand and give away her own shaken emotions.

'Some people compensate by marrying for companionship,' he said. '*Merci*, sugar but no cream.'

'Will you have some more orange juice, Desi?' She hoped to change the trend of the conversation, for it had now become rather intolerable to speak of such things with Paul, to whom marriage could never have the meaning it might have had if Satancourt had been his inheritance instead of Michel's. She had learned that night up on the terraces that he would not be averse to a love affair; but such an *affaire* could only break her heart as his mother's had been broken. She would not go through that sort of agony, not even for Paul. She would sooner go away . . . walk away as Michel had walked away from her. Yes, perhaps that was what she must do before long ... before his arms should ever close round her again. Next time the strength would not be there to deny him, or herself. She glanced away from his hard brown arms, dark-haired against the rolled sleeves of his white shirt.

'I am all filled up.' Desi patted his small stomach appreciatively. 'Uncle Paul, do you think that I grow bigger every day so that soon I shall be as big as you?'

'I am sure, *mon enfant*, that it will not take too long for you to become a much bigger man than I.' Paul drew the boy between his knees and studied the young face that was a replica of his brother's. 'Do you want to miss your lessons this morning and ride to the mill with me to watch the small casks being rinsed out on the new machine up there? I am sure you will enjoy seeing the water being jetted in through the bungholes, eh?'

The boy turned eager eyes to Margo. 'May I go to see this, *mademoiselle*, and not do lessons this morning?'

'I am sure your uncle feels, Desi, that it will be educational for you to get to know all the processes of the family business.' She smiled at him, and yet her heart quickened with the strangest twinge of anxiety. 'If you wish to go to the mill then *bien*, but don't get in the way of any of the machinery—'

'I shall ensure that Desi comes to no harm – with me.' Paul spoke curtly and rose to his feet, swinging Desi to his shoulders with easy, almost dangerous strength. His eyes met Margo's and they glinted with mocking awareness of what lay behind her plea that Desi take care up there in the mill. 'Perhaps you would like to come also, to make sure I don't let him wander where he shouldn't?'

Her cheeks burned ... how could she love him and think him a devil at the same time? How could she think he would harm Desi when she knew he loved the boy?

Yet love had various depths, and deep in Paul's bones lay his love for Satancourt!

She wanted to trust him ... and then with a shrug he turned away from her and carried off his nephew to the steps that led down to the hall of the chateau. Desi turned and waved to her and then they were gone, and up on the roof patio it was quiet but for the cicadas who were ever present and yet always unseen ... like the motives in the human heart.

The peach which Paul had plucked lay on the table untouched, and Margo pressed a hand against her throat as if to ease the pain she felt there. She loved him ... oh yes, she loved him, and yet again she had looked and spoken like a woman who hated him.

Margo decided to spend the morning in her sitting-room. She had some mending to catch up with, a couple of letters to write, and a little thinking to do.

She was crossing the hall when she ran into Yvonne Dalbert. She was about to say *bonjour* and walk on when the other girl detained her. 'Where is the boy?' she asked. 'Is it not time for his lessons?'

'He has gone with M'sieur Paul to the wine terraces,' Margo explained, feeling again that sense of animosity which lay in every glance, every word spoken to her by Madame's companion.

'How popular are the wine terraces just lately,' Yvonne remarked insinuatingly. 'I wonder what it is about them that draws governess and pupil like a magnet? Could it be the man in charge of them, do you think?'

Margo hung on to her composure and would not be angered by this second cousin of the family, who behind Madame's back was far from the deferential person she appeared in front of Paul and his mother. There was insolence and dislike in the way she was looking at Margo, who stood where a shaft of sunlight came through one of the lancet windows and lit her hair, merging with the dark red of it to create a sort of nimbus. Her skin by contrast was pale and her eyes a dark violet.

'You don't fool me.' said Yvonne, and hatred flashed into her eyes, made all the more venomous by the glitter of her glasses. 'I know you were up there with Paul the other night. When you didn't appear for dinner I went and took a look into his study . . . you see Berthe sometimes leaves her keys in her room when she has the evening off and Jean takes her across to the mainland. That evening she was absent, so I borrowed her keys and unlocked the door of the study. I had an idea he was with you. Like his brother he has a side to him — well, let us say that he likes his fun now and then, especially with a woman he has no intention of marrying!'

'How dare you say that!' Margo was inflamed by the spiteful, spying character of this sallow creature who could not attract Paul herself. 'I wonder if you would dare to say it to Madame?'

'Why not?' drawled Yvonne. 'I am sure she would be most interested to hear that you go to the terraces with him — to make love!'

'We did no such thing! Paul wished to show me the vines by moonlight, and it is just like your spiteful mind to make up tales you would like to happen to yourself. You implied that that other girl died in the lake. You wanted to blacken Paul, make me as a newcomer distrust him. Why, Mademoiselle Dalbert? Why do you hate him? What has he ever done to you? I have never seen him anything but polite towards you — or is that the trouble? You would prefer him to be impolite, rough with you, aware of you as a female rather than a relative of his mother's?'

'You will not say such things to me.' Yvonne's voice rose with sudden passionate anger. 'You are the one who is after him! You think to raise yourself from the position of governess to that of a rich man's wife — or mistress! The irony of it, Mademoiselle Jones, is that Paul Cassalis is as much an employee here as you or I. Everything will go to the boy when he is of age – if he lives that long! I think that Paul will get rid of him as he got rid of Desi's father. Ah yes, it was always partially true that someone died in the lake at his hands, only it wasn't that stupid girl, it was his brother Michel. He tampered with the engine of the boat – I saw him! Yes, I saw him the night before the accident, at the boathouse where Michel's boat was kept. I was taking a walk – it was a moonlit night, and with my own eyes I saw him emerge from the boathouse – and next day when the engine exploded and Michel was killed I knew that Paul had fixed it so that the speedboat would explode. He knew, as everyone knew, that Michael was mad about fast cars, fast boats – and fast women!'

There was a deadly silence in the hall after Yvonne had flung these words at Margo ... she was still flinching from them, still denying their possible truth when Yvonne swung on her heel and walked away. Margo was vaguely aware that she made for the baize door that led to the kitchen; as it swung open and then closed behind the thin, dark-clad figure, Margo sank back against the baluster of the stairs, and there was no denying that she had seen some sort of awful truth in the eyes of Yvonne Dalbert. She had seen Paul coming from the boathouse that night ... and he, above all, was the one person at Satancourt who had reason to hate Michel ... who had cause to hate anyone who stood in the way of his ownership of the chateau and the wine terraces. If Desi should die, then the property would revert to the hands of Lucien Cassalis' widow – Paul's mother.

Through her, and her alone, could Paul become legal master of his nephew's inheritance.

CHAPTER TEN

MARGO went up to her room, but once there she found that she was too restless to sit down to sewing or letter writing. Yvonne and the things she had said had stirred awake those doubts of Paul, those dark imaginings, that memory of being with him in the *salon* and thinking that he was like a devil in a silver room.

The remembrance of that moment jarred through her ... was it then that she had come to love him, even as she doubted him, even as she wondered if he had a heart to match his black hair and his sun-blackened skin?

She wandered on to her balcony and stood gazing at the dense green of the wine terraces above which rose the broad white sails of the windmill. Overhead the sky was a rather cloudy blue and the earlier burst of sunshine had faded; the brightness was gone but the sultriness remained. Nothing seemed to stir except the sails of the windmill; nothing seemed alive but Margo's heart, beating with a sort of heavy anxiety, as if she waited for those awful words of Yvonne Dalbert's to be proved.

But she couldn't wait! She couldn't just stand here and let happen to Desi what had happened to Michel!

The next moment she was wrenching open the door of her suite and running along the gallery to the stairs. At the bend she collided with someone, a hard, lean figure whose hands caught at her and brought her to a halt.

'What is this?' Raoul demanded. 'You are running, Margo, as if the chateau is on fire. What is the matter?'

'I – I have allowed Desi to go to the terraces and now I am going to fetch him. He has been up there long enough and it looks as if it might rain.'

'Margo, there is fear in your eyes! For a drop of rain?'

Raoul stared at her face. 'Come, the boy won't drown. Come with me and let me finish that sketch of you which I started the other day.'

His calmness and reasonableness quietened her fears. She was allowing that Dalbert girl to upset her, and probably for no reason. Yvonne was jealous of anyone Paul looked at, and ready to say anything to discredit him because he treated her kindly but impersonally. Margo had to believe this or go crazy.

'You're right, of course,' she said to Raoul. 'I am being a fool, but when I saw the sky clouding over I thought of those quick fierce storms that now and then hit this part of the country—'

'And you fear for the child who has lost his father, eh?' Raoul smiled understandingly, and then shot a glance at his wristwatch. 'It is just after eleven o'clock and the perfect hour for drinking a glass of the best champagne. It is what you need, Margo, to settle your unsettled nerves. I have the feeling something – or someone – has upset you. Am I right?'

'No—' She shrugged and could not tell him what Yvonne had said about Paul. Raoul was loyal . . . far more so than she, whose love for Paul was shot through by doubts . . . by the bleak awareness that she meant no more to him than a passing attraction. "I – I believe I could do with a glass of champagne.' She made herself speak gaily. 'It seems terribly decadent to drink it in the morning, but if you are offering, *m'sieur*, then I am accepting.'

'Good for you!' He swept an arm about her waist and escorted her down the stairs to the hall; they passed that place near the stairs where the French girl had accused Paul of tampering with his brother's boat, and Margo's heart began to ache again. If only she knew the truth! If only she could go to Paul and find the courage to ask him if he had been in the boathouse that night preceding the fatal accident. His presence there could have been totally innocent, bearing no relation to Michel's boat and what had gone wrong with it. The wreckage would have been examined after the tragedy and surely the police would have discovered signs of misuse.

'Raoul,' she paused to face him, and now the hall was shadowed as the day outside gradually darkened. 'Were you here – when Michel died?'

He shook his head. 'I was abroad on business, but I hurried here as soon as I heard the news. At first Maxine was critically ill and we thought she would die, but by the mercy of *le bon Dieu* she recovered. Are you still wondering if it was altogether an accident?'

'I – I'm afraid so,' she admitted.

'I am certain that it was.' Raoul opened the door of the *salon* and Margo entered the lovely, silvery room, with its tapestries and silk chairs and beautifully figured mirrors. She looked aound her . . . the silver room in which Paul's *diablerie* had seemed so potent. Was he a devil, or was he a strange sort of saint who strove to make the chateau and its wine the perfect things they were for the sake of merely loving them?

She walked to a window and stood looking out; gone was that pure white light of high summer, with the heat burning in the sky like a flame. She knew in all her nerves that a storm threatened, and it was bringing out strongly the scents of the earth, of the dark roses in the garden, and the raspberries among the brambles.

The *jardin de norblaize*, she thought, with a catch in her throat. He loved those, she knew, almost more than the vine flowers and their unforgettable scent.

From here, as Raoul took champagne from the cooler built inside the wine cabinet, she could see a tower of the chateau, stone piled on stone, leaf hung upon leaf to mantle its walls, rising up in a dark lordly way to its conical rooftop, set with four narrow, diamond-paned windows, behind which an enchanter might cast his dark spells and set loose dark desires.

She heard the sigh of the champagne cork as Raoul opened the bottle, and she turned to watch as he poured the wine into long-stemmed, tulip-shaped glasses. The conventional *coupe*, with its wide mouth and its legend of having been fashioned from the breast of Helen, was never used at Satancourt. Paul always declared that the bouquet of the wine was lost in such a glass and retained only in the tulip-glass.

'Would you like with this a chicken sandwich?' Raoul asked. 'The two go perfectly together.'

'No, I'm not hungry. *Merci, m'sieur.*' She took the glass he held out to her, and she agitated the bubbles so that she might see them rise through the clear gold wine. 'When I was a poor girl working in a flower shop I would never have believed that I would drink champagne in a silver room, at this hour of the day.'

Raoul sipped his wine and gave her a quizzical look. 'I won't believe that you are a conventional person,' he said. 'Your face is too intriguing for that, and your hair holds a dark flame. Your eyes, also, are an unusual shade of blue, and as an artist I am fascinated by unusual people. Tell me, Margo, are you fascinated by Paul?'

She was startled and the tulip of champagne almost slipped from her hand. She knew that Raoul's eyes narrowed. He had noticed her start, and the indication this gave of the cause of her nervousness. 'I – I wonder about him,' she confessed.

'He is not the usual sort of *vendangeur*, is he?'

She shook her head and sipped the delicious wine produced from the clear green grapes grown up there on a wide flank of the terraces. The wine ran through her veins, sweet and cool like the ripplings of a harp, and because she feared to look at Raoul, who was shrewd, she lifted her gaze to the lovely old chandeliers, of such a clear crystal as to have a sheen of silver on their clusters of lights.

'*Ma doue!* You think him a little satanic, eh? To match this place; this shadow on silver; this chateau that sees forever its reflection in a lake, almost a dream – or do you think it holds nightmare?'

Then she looked at him; she had to. A wild protest was in her eyes, that he should guess, that he should know what shadowed the beauty of this place for her.

'It would be absurd for one fool in love to offer advice to another,' he said, and his expression was very wry and Gallic in that moment. 'Shall we each have another glass of wine and let our troubles be stolen away for a while?'

'Why not?' She handed him her empty glass and tried not to let it matter too much that he had guessed her secret, perhaps with the intuition of a man in love himself with someone who did not return his love. 'But I hope we are not plundering the family's *vins de cachet.*'

'We probably are,' he smiled, but it seemed not to worry him as he poured more of the wine into their glasses. After that they wandered about the *salon* looking at the tapestries which he said were perfect works of art, each flower, each leaf, each feature of the faces as finely worked as true art could make a thing. 'Wonderful,' he breathed. 'It makes my own work seem humble by comparison, but in this modern age the finer details are no longer required. Bold faces are called pretty when they are really just healthy and ordinary. Lank hair romps about the shoulders of these earthy wenches, and large hips are displayed by the tight trousers, and there is not a bit of mystery for a man to enjoy. Perhaps you and I, Margo, should have lived in the Renaissance days. You have the hair and the looks for it, and I have the appreciation. To escape from reality would suit us both, I think.'

'Do you really believe that?' She gave him a candid

look. 'I sense that you would like nothing better than to — to make a life with the woman you care for.'

'I won't argue with you.' He sat down on one of the love-seats and leaned his arm on the back of it. He studied Margo there against the silken sweep of the curtains, their paleness a foil for her dark-flame hair and the fawn-coloured uniform which she wore. 'Do you plan to stay here, Margo, or do I sense that you find it a trial to stay under the same roof with Paul? Are you afraid of him, or is it yourself you are really afraid of?'

'What a strange question, Raoul. Why should I be afraid of myself?'

'Because you are basically a young puritan, and yet you feel yourself physically drawn to this man — ah, don't deny it, *petite*. I am too much a man of the world to be fooled. I know the devastating effect that such a man can have on a girl who is pure yet who has a warm temperament. No one can deny that Michel Cassalis had charm — but it is Paul who has the sexual fascination. It permeates through his very skin, and when I worked alongside him in the vineyards of Brittany I saw how the grape-pickers would look at him, so dark and powerful, and yet curiously aloof. He could have any one of them, at any time of the hot, grape-gathering day, but always the work came first with him. He thrives on it as the grape thrives on the sun; as the vine relishes the deep dark earth. He is a passionate man, but the women in his life have been mere playthings, noticed for an hour and then forgotten. You fear to become one of these women — is this not so?'

She shuddered ... it was as if a bleak cold wind passed over her. When Michel had walked out on her it had hurt, but she didn't dare to think of what it would do to her to be discarded by Paul. That must never happen. And to prevent it happening she must inevitably leave Satancourt.

'I always thought, *m'sieur*, that champagne made a person feel gay instead of introspective.' She forced a smile to her lips. 'Do you plan to return soon to Paris?'

'Yes, my work is there.' A sigh caught at him. 'Why not come with me, Margo? You could be my model for a while. I like your proud young head and the shape of your bones. It could be a sound working arrangement – with no strings attached, Miss Jones, to set your mind at rest.'

Her smile became easier, more genuine. 'It would be nice to see Paris again,' she said. 'I might think over your proposition, *m'sieur*. Don't they say that if your heart cannot be mended in Paris it will never mend at all?'

'I think you are what the British call a brave sport, Margo.' He rose and came over to her and placed an arm lightly about her waist; he turned her so they faced the window and she saw tiny specks of rain in the panes of glass.

'The rain has started,' she said. 'I hope it doesn't pelt down. I am told that the grapevines prefer the hot sun to the cool rain.'

'Yes,' he agreed. 'As the time draws near for the gathering the skin of the grapes grows very fine and if the rain should be a fierce one, many of the grapes will be damaged and litres of wine be lost. Paul needs a good profit for the upkeep of the chateau, for in this age of high taxation family fortunes do not last as long as they did in days gone by. I think without Paul this whole place would have gone to slow ruin in the past fifteen years. Michel went fast through the money left to him by his father, and it is an irony that *his* son should inherit what Paul has saved and served.'

'Raoul—?'

'Yes, *petite*?' He glanced down at her. 'Ask away.'

'Do you think if Michel had lived he would eventually have sold all this – disposed of it to reimburse his dissipated fortune?'

'It is very possible – perhaps almost inevitable. He always needed money to pay for his pleasures, and though Maxine brought to him a fairly good dowry, her father's remarriage ensured that he would not be so ready to put his hand in his pocket.'

'Then—' the doubts and the fears rose again to almost stop the beat of Margo's heart, 'it is also possible that Paul might have become desperate enough to do anything to save Satancourt from being sold out of the family? He and Michel were only half-brothers. They had little in common, and there is a passion in Paul for this place. A passion beyond what he feels for people. From a boy he has loved every stone of the chateau, every grapevine up there on the terraces. Such a love could almost excuse him—' She broke off painfully, and felt the sudden grip of Raoul's fingers against her waist. He swung her round to face him and in his eyes she saw the same painful searching that must be in her eyes.

'How,' he demanded, 'how can you care for that man and yet fear to leave that child alone with him? Heaven knows if Michel died by accident or not, but don't persuade me to believe that Paul would ever harm the boy. He has great affection for the little one – you have seen it – I have seen it. Maxine's son—' Raoul's words died away and he and Margo were staring at each other as the room visibly darkened and then was shockingly lit by a fierce flash of lightning. Every nerve in Margo's body seemed to respond sickeningly to the flash ... the silent, sinister lightning of a storm following extremely hot weather.

'I – I must go and fetch Desi.' She broke from Raoul and made for the door. She was wrenching at the handle when he reached her side ... she was struggling with it, but it wouldn't turn. 'Raoul!'

'Let me try.' He was even more urgent, and when the door wouldn't open he thrust a shoulder against it, but the timber was thick and strong and the hinges of solid brass. 'This door is locked, Margo. Someone has turned the key – how very strange!'

'We must get out!' she said, and all the anxiety of the morning was suddenly a weight of fear that made her stumble as she raced to the windows which here in the *salon* were gracious bays overlooking a drop to the garden. A fairly steep drop, for the garden below was reached by steps from the courtyard itself.

'Raoul,' she swung to face him as that soundless lightning lit the gloom of the room, 'I know Desi is in danger. I feel it. We must get out of here before the child is hurt—' She couldn't say the word that was in her mind, flaring there as the lightning flared. But Raoul saw it written in her eyes, and quickly he flung open a casement of the bay window and he stared down at the garden, with its flowering shrubs set round a lawn, where Madame Cassalis sometimes sat with a book. Now it was empty and the smell of the storm and the wet grass were strong on the air.

'It is too far to jump.' Raoul spoke decisively. 'I am going to thump that locked door with a chair and I am going to hope that someone hears the noise and has a key with which to open the door.' He picked up one of the silk-brocaded chairs as he spoke and proceeded to thump the door with it. Each thump seemed echoed by Margo's heart, while her thoughts flew to Paul and she prayed that she was wrong . . . wrong about her terrible suspicion that he had killed Michel and now, possibly with his mother's help in locking this door, he meant to do away with Desi. It was true that he loved the boy . . . but wasn't Satancourt his own life? Its grace and isolation and blue-green terraces the promise of his own youth which the father of Michel had snatched from his hands with a few curt words in the testament a lawyer had probably read without emotion an hour after Lucien Cassalis had been laid to rest beneath the dark soil and the white lilies.

'Someone has heard!'

A hand was agitating the outside handle of the door and they heard voices, that of a woman, high and flurried, and that of a man ... a deep rumble, possibly Hercule, brought from the kitchen by Berthe.

'Berthe will have her keys!' Margo clutched at Raoul's arm, and they waited tensely as various keys were tried in the lock, until it became apparent that the exact key to the door of the *salon* was missing from the housekeeper's *chatelaine*.

'This door has to be opened!' Raoul shouted. 'It's imperative!'

A consultation seemed to go on beyond the door, and then Margo felt sure she heard someone running. She glanced at Raoul, whose lean face was strained, who had obviously caught from her the anxious fear that Desi was in danger. She knew what Raoul was thinking. If anything should happen to the boy, then Maxine would give up altogether the struggle to get well and start a new life.

Margo gave a jump as something of iron was thrust into the lock of the door. A strong arm was behind the thrust, for there was a grinding sound as the lock gave; the handle was turned and the door opened to reveal Hercule in shirt sleeves, a poker in his hands, and beside him Berthe ... and Madame Cassalis!

Madame looked directly at Margo. 'How did you come to be locked in?' she demanded. 'How did it happen? Berthe cannot find the key on her chain, so the lock had to be broken. I gave the order.'

Margo could only gaze at Paul's mother with rather stricken eyes ... eyes that pleaded, questioned, wondered, and then she was running across the hall towards the covered walk, with its archways leading out to the courtyard. The rain came at her as she made for the stables, and her uniform was plastered to her by the time she reached the stall in which stood the young mare which Céleste often rode. It would take too long to get to the terraces on foot, and Margo was feverishly saddling the horse when Raoul came hurrying in.

'Yes, ride up there.' He held the stirrup while she mounted somewhat awkwardly because of her skirt. There was a sound of a tearing seam and her light leg was bared as she caught at the reins, gave Raoul an eloquent look and turned her mount's head to the yard.

'I will be right behind you,' Raoul promised. 'But, Margo—'

'Yes?' Her look was now impatient; she wanted to be off, to find and face the devil that was Paul . . . for there was a devil up there at the wine terraces, her every nerve and instinct told her, and it wasn't only for the sake of Desi that she was driven up there. It was love or hate that was her spur, and she didn't yet know for sure which emotion dominated.

'Paul could not have locked that door,' Raoul said, and lightning zig-zagged into the stable and a horse in the next stall whinnied nervously.

'I know,' she said, her hands clenching on the reins. 'But Madame was there in the house, and I know that behind that cold mask on her face there is suffering, bitter reproach that she caused Paul to be disinherited. I believe she would do anything he asked of her . . . especially if he asked her to keep me away from him!'

Then, slapping her hand against the horse's neck, she was off, and thunder rumbled as the hooves of the animal clattered on the cobbles of the yard. They were wet, slippery, and it wasn't until Margo glimpsed through the driving rain the path to the terraces that she gave the horse a free rein. The mare was slender and swift, her small ears laid flat in fear of the lightning as it licked over the lake and cast a blue-white light over the hanging vines. They dripped with moisture at either side of Margo, and her hair hung in a wet tangle to her shoulders as she urged the mare up the slope to the spread soils of the windmill. The lower half of the mill was now used for the crushing and bottling of the vintage, in the upper part was the wheel that turned the sails and where the wicker grape baskets were stored, piled up waiting for the day when they would be carried down to the yard and aired in the sun for the gathering of the wine grapes.

It was the kind of place in which any small adventurous boy would love to play ... it was also the kind of place where anything could happen very easily and be called an accident.

Margo had almost reached the terraces when another of those violent flashes lit the landscape and she involuntarily closed her eyes and crouched in the saddle as if expecting to be struck. She heard a distinct crackling and almost at once she smelled smoke, and when she opened her eyes she saw with horror that flame was licking at the sails of the windmill and they were smouldering darkly, while a red flare was leaping beyond the windows of the mill, with its woodwork and its beams, its piles of inflammable baskets and its twisting timber stairs.

With the taste of fear and smoke in her mouth she brought the mare to a standstill and her uniform ripped again as she climbed from the saddle. She ran among the vines towards the burning windmill, and shreds of the still turning sails were flying down on the vines and the men who were running from the terraces where they had been working. The tall figure of Paul could not be seen among them, and the fire was gaining a wild hold on the interior of the mill.

Smoke and flame gushed from the openings of the mill, and the sound of the fire mingled with the thunder of the storm and added a nightmare quality to the scene.

Margo reached the yard and ran to one of the workers.

'Where is the child?' She caught urgently at his arm. 'Is he with M'sieur Paul?'

'They must be in there!' He gestured at the burning mill. 'The boss was showing the small one how everything worked — I saw them together myself about twenty minutes ago. Look, the flames are coming out of the front door, which means that the stairs must now be alight!'

'We must get to them! Have you no hoses, no fire-fighting equipment?' Margo could feel the sting of sparks as she and the workman stood beneath the blackened swing of the sails.

'The hoses are in the storeroom.' His gesture held despair. 'We are always careful. M'sieur forbids smoking in there, and only *le bon Dieu* could know that the devil would strike it with lightning.'

'Was it the lightning?' The words leapt from her lips even as flame leapt from the doorway and the narrow windows set in the tower-like structure of the windmill. Something crashed inside and as smoke billowed into the yard everyone retreated from the raining sparks and pieces of debris.

Margo wanted to rush inside, regardless of the flames, and discover for herself if Paul was in there and Desi with him. This wild urgency must have showed itself in her eyes, for fingers caught at her arm and the man beside her held her back from the smoke and the blowing ashes which the rain quenched as it could not quench her terrible fear and her love for Paul.

'Let me go to him!'

She spoke the words almost without being aware of speaking them aloud, and the fingers tightened on her arm until they made bruises.

'*Mademoiselle*, there is nothing anyone can do! The whole place is afire and the upper part is an inferno, filled as it is with those baskets! See you — the roof is going!'

They all backed away again, crossing themselves as the

roof gave and pieces of burning timber fell into the yard. Margo felt as if her whole life was turning into ruins, and with a deadly white face she pulled free of the workman's grip and turned to run from the holocaust before she ran into it.

'*Mademoiselle!*'

The childish voice rang out in the silence gripping the men, above the crackling of the flames. A high, excited, yet frightened voice. And the next moment a small figure hurled itself from among the terraced vines and ran on swift legs to Margo. She caught him to her, holding him hard to make sure he was real and living and unhurt. 'Desi – darling! Where have you been? Oh, I've been so worried about you!' The words could not express what she had really feared ... what she still feared. 'Where is your uncle? Where is Paul?'

Desi clenched his arms about her and stared past her at the windmill wreathed in flames. His eyes were huge and wondering; fearful and yet fascinated.

'Paul?' Only his name would now scrape out of her smoke-dried throat.

'I am here, *mon amour*.' The deep voice spoke directly behind her, and there was only one voice like it in the whole world ... but was it of this world?

Her legs were shaking and her heart was pounding when she turned to look, and then Margo Jones did something she had never done before in her life ... she fainted at the feet of a man.

They talked about it long afterwards, the folk of the island and those who lived across the lake in the Loire valley, how the Big Man carried the English girl down the wine terraces to the chateau, all the way in his arms, with the boy running at his side and not caring that the mill burned to the ground and many of the vines were lost when the smoke and the hot ashes blew over them.

His face, they said, had not looked so gentle and caring for years, not since the day of his youth when he called Lucien Cassalis his father. And not once did he glance back to see what became of his precious vines.

The English girl awoke in his arms when they reached the chateau, where his mother waited for them, wearing over her silver hair that had once been as shining and darkly red as the girl's the black lace scarf of her widowhood. Her only words for several moment's were: 'Paul, my son!' And then she told them that Berthe had found the key of the *salon* in Yvonne's bedroom, but they couldn't find her. Was she up at the mill? Raoul would have gone to look, but Maxine had to be pacified when she had seen the fire and feared for her son.

'Desi,' Madame Cassalis released the child's hand, which she had been holding tightly in her own, 'go to your *maman* and let her see that you are alive and well.'

He ran off, and when Margo whispered to Paul that he let her out of his arms, he shook his head and held her tightly as he and his mother looked at the beacon that was the mill. 'Why,' he asked, 'did Yvonne have the key of the *salon*?'

'She locked Margo in there, with Raoul, and we had to break the lock.' His mother caught at his arm. 'She knew you had taken the boy to the mill – Paul, how did the fire start?'

'I am not certain, Maman, to tell you the truth. I was with Desi at the small memorial on the terrace where we grow Lucien's champagne grapes. The little stone, remember, that we put there in the place where he died that hot day, his heart failing him because he would help with the first gathering of his beautiful golden-green grapes. I wished the child to understand the love of land and the loyalty to what it can be made to yield. We were there, and I was talking to him about his grandfather when we saw the lightning, and almost simultaneously the fire. Maman, what are you thinking?'

'Paul,' his mother's face was white and drawn, 'it is my fault that Yvonne is bitter. I – I promised her that she would be your wife – I said I would arrange it, and then Mademoiselle Jones came to Satancourt.' The shrug which Madame Cassalis gave was significant, and also the look which took in the girl in her son's arms. 'I think Yvonne went to the terraces to cause trouble. She must still be up there – Paul, she may have been trapped in the mill!'

Margo shuddered and buried her face in Paul's shoulder. She and the men up there had sensed that someone was in the mill. They had thought it was Paul ... but thanks to heaven he was here, strong and alive and holding her as if he meant never to let her go again.

'You must rest,' he murmured. 'And I must go back up there for a while.'

He carried her into the hall of the chateau, and there she insisted on being set upon her feet. They didn't speak; he merely touched her cheek with his hand, and then he left her to return to the blackened mill.

Margo was resting on her bed, half asleep, when there was a tap on her bedroom door and she called out 'Entrez,' in a sleepy voice. The door opened and Berthe came into the room. She was carrying a small tray and she brought it to the side of the bed. 'Coffee and cognac, mademoiselle. I was told to bring it to you by Madame.'

Margo sat up and reached for the cup. 'Thank you, Berthe.' She sipped the delicious brew, and her eyes dwelt with silent inquiry on the housekeeper's face. 'Is there any news, Berthe? About—?'

Berthe inclined her head, with its neatly coiled grey hair, 'M'sieur Raoul found her in the rose garden, of all places, composedly reading a novel! And quickly, before

M'sieur Paul arrived back from the terraces, he packed her off in Jean's boat. She admitted nothing, but I was with Madame when Raoul told her that the girl gave a spiteful laugh as she stepped into the boat. He said that she—' Berthe broke off, biting her lip.

'Go on.' Margo's face was very pale against the copper gleam of her hair. 'Tell me everything.'

'She cursed you, *mademoiselle*.'

'Me – not *M'sieur*?'

'You, *mademoiselle*.'

Margo relaxed against her pillows and a faint smile touched her lips. 'I think, Berthe, that as the great-great-granddaughter of a Welsh witch I shall survive the curse of Mademoiselle Dalbert. Was it the lightning, I wonder, that struck the windmill?'

'If it was, they will find thunderstones in the ruins. If not—'

The woman and the girl looked at each other for a long silent moment, then Margo finished her coffee and returned the cup to the tray. 'How is Desi's mother?' she asked.

'She is with her son right now, *mademoiselle*. And M'sieur Raoul is with both of them.'

'Good.' Margo's smile deepened. 'I think I might sleep for an hour or two, if I am not wanted by anyone.'

Berthe smiled herself as she made for the door. 'I think you will be wanted before the day is out, *mademoiselle*.' The door closed behind the housekeeper and the keys could be heard rattling on her *chatelaine* as she walked away. Margo buried her face in her pillow, trying to cool the sudden deep flush in her cheeks. She knew to whom Berthe referred ... her heart and her body knew who she wanted.

And later that night, while smoke from the fire still haunted the air, Margo stood with Paul on the roof patio and they watched the stars in the storm-washed sky, shining and clear above the pinnacles of the chateau.

Paul stirred and looked at her, and her arms slipped of themselves about his neck and her fingers buried themselves in his thick black hair. A breeze rustled and the scent of roses came on the night air, mingling with the smoke as doubt had mingled in Margo's heart with her love for Paul.

'How do I say I'm sorry?' she whispered. 'How do I make up to you for what I believed? Yvonne told me you were in the boathouse the night before your brother's accident. She said – oh, Paul, she said you tampered with the engine of Michel's boat!'

'I was there,' he admitted, a black brow wryly twisted, 'but it never entered my head to touch the boat. I wanted some oil to take up to the mill for the cogs of the wheel, that is all. I never keep oil on the premises of the mill—' He broke off and his arms tightened about her. 'I go on living and thinking in the past, but it is just a habit with me. From now on I put *our* lives before anything else. I cease from this moment to be the eternally vigilant *vigneron*.'

'But, Paul,' she laid a hand across his lips, 'I wouldn't want you to be other than what you are. To be a *vigneron* is your life, and I would share it, if you wished – if you needed me – if you asked—'

'Need I ask?' he murmured, his lips against the side of her smooth cool neck. 'Can't you feel how much I wish, how much I need, how much I long to have you? From the first moment we looked at each other a thousand nights began for us, a thousand dreams seemed possible. I never wanted a woman who would melt at my touch, but one who would take fire.' Suddenly he was kissing her, and the terrifying love-violence of his kisses made her tremble, and burn. Suddenly there was danger in his arms, and there was shelter, and a wonderful excitement. Suddenly all loneliness was gone and she could surrender herself, her life, all her future, into the keeping of this man ... not quite an angel, but not altogether a devil.

His hands held her face to the starlight, and her copper hair tumbled over his fingers, the rough, strong, clever fingers of the born *vigneron*.

'There has not been a bride like you at Satancourt for years and years,' he said exultantly.

'Darling, I am not yet a bride.' Her heart beat furiously at the look in his eyes. And pulling her to him, hugging her to his heart, he laughed, and somewhere in the trees a night bird fluttered its wings.

'How I love you, Margo.' Paul's voice was strong and warm with love. 'My passionate puritan!'